WILD SUMMER

by

James DuBern

Published in 2020 by Amazon KDP Publishing.

This is a work of fiction. Names, characters, places, and incidents either are the products of the author's imagination or are used fictitiously. Any resemblance to actual persons, living or dead, businesses, companies, events, or locales is entirely coincidental.

Cover illustration © Kateryna Kirdoglo. All rights reserved.

Paperback formatting and copy editing by Naomi Munts Proofreading.

Contents

Chapter 1

Cobra on the Loose

Mariella led a trio of visitors – mum, dad and their daughter – across her farmyard. The mother of the family, in immaculate white trainers, stepped dramatically around puddles as if they might explode. Her husband caught her glances and tutted, hoisting their daughter onto his shoulders. Mariella, with messy brown hair and a rich tan from working outside all summer, remained oblivious. She splashed happily through her domain in well-worn red wellies. The group reached a stable cobbled together from wooden planks and plywood sheets.

"This is Barney," Mariella said, affectionately stroking the donkey's muzzle. "We rescued him from Devon, where he was too weak to continue carrying children on beach rides. He had a bad leg and was limping. You can see from this photograph that they still worked him hard despite Barney being in considerable pain."

Next to the stable door was a framed photograph of a donkey on a beach, looking defeated with his head hung low. Despite his misery, a queue of children and their parents snaked from the donkey to the edge of the photo. It was a heartbreaking scene of a neglected and overworked animal, struggling in the relentless sun.

The family stared at it and the mother began to get emotional, pulling her daughter close and sniffing to hold back the tears. Finally she broke the silence.

"Look at that, Dave. Just look at it. Makes you want to get in the car right now and go to Spain, dunnit?"

Mariella swung her head around to check she was hearing her right.

"Beautiful!" her husband added. "I think that's Greek islands, though. And there's a little donkey for Ashleigh to ride. We should get a picture like that at our house. Maybe Photoshop the donkey though. It's a bit tatty, ain't it?"

Mariella stood there in disbelief. "It's in Devon, that beach, not Greece. And like I said, they worked poor Barney into the ground and we were called in to take care of him in his old age. Often a donkey will be put down when it can no longer make money for its owners, which is really sad."

The guy piped up, eager to show off his business acumen. "Right, but now Benji is going to be making money for you."

Mariella breathed slowly to calm herself, before responding as diplomatically as she could. "It's Barney, from Devon. See; it says it there. He doesn't generate profit. None of our donkeys do. It costs a lot of money to feed them and we don't even charge an entry fee, only ask for donations. I think you can see that we're not exactly rolling in it."

He shrugged and his wife eventually chimed in, breaking the awkward silence. "Ashleigh's got something to ask. Go on, Ash. Say it to the lady."

The young girl was about seven years old but looked older because she wore lipstick, presumably to match her mum. She groaned loudly

9

at the impending chore of having to talk to a grown-up, then pointed to Barney.

"I wanna ride that 'orse."

Mariella crouched to break the bad news to Ashleigh.

"I'm afraid we don't offer donkey rides because our animals are almost all with us because they can't do that anymore. You can pet Barney though, or I can show you some of our other donkeys if you'd like that?"

"Your zoo sucks," she responded matter-of-factly, folding her arms.

Mariella was taken aback by her rudeness and wondered if her parents would step in, but they clearly agreed.

Suddenly the loudspeaker system crackled into life and emitted a painful squeal of feedback. A strangely nasal voice came over the park, and the group looked up in unison at the source of the sound.

"This is a customer announcement. We regret to inform you that a cobra has escaped from its enclosure and is loose in the park. Please return to your vehicles as soon as possible. Repeat. A COBRA is currently on the loose in this park and you need to leave now."

The mum screamed and immediately darted across the yard towards the entrance, mud splashing up her white jeans as she ran hysterically. The dad picked up his daughter heroically and ran after her, shouting back at Mariella: "A donkey you can't ride. Now a cobra on the loose? What the hell kind of business are you running, you mad woman?"

And with that, they were gone.

Chapter 2

D-E-V-O-N

It dried up by the afternoon and turned into a gorgeous July evening. Spread over 25 acres, Cranmore Donkey Sanctuary was a scattering of buildings around a concrete yard, surrounded by seven large fields. The property had evolved over the years with necessity as its only architect. Stables had been added and extended as new donkeys arrived. A large pond had been excavated to encourage wildlife and a vegetable patch had sprung into life when money was tight. Everything was wonky and the buildings were a mishmash of whatever materials were to hand when they had been hammered into place. In fact, the only structure with straight lines was the Portakabin that served as both the office and visitor centre, and even that had been plonked at a strange angle that lined up with nothing else. Beyond the stables and the yard there was a small bungalow in which Mariella lived with her twelve-year-old daughter Rosie.

To visitors it was nothing more than a ramshackle patchwork of workshops and stables, packed with braying donkeys and a white horse. To Mariella and Rosie, it was paradise.

Between Rosie's brain and her mum's fantastic ability to build and fix things, they were able to make anything they wanted. Rosie had taken the electronics out of a cat feeder and was in the middle of building it into a carrot dispenser to serve treats to her beloved donkeys while she was at school. In fact, there was only one thing this duo couldn't make, and that was money.

It was a good thing that Rosie was uninterested in spending her weekends at the shops like most of her classmates. She cared little about clothes and, like her mum, tended to throw on denim shorts and whatever t-shirt was on the top of the pile. That evening she wore cut-off dungarees over a stripy blue t-shirt. The sun was setting as she cleaned out the stables with her mum, and it took longer than normal because they kept stopping to reminisce about their afternoon.

"Seriously, I need you to start again from the beginning. It's. Just. SO. Good!" Mariella said.

"Okay, okay," said Rosie, stabbing her pitchfork into a bale of hay and sitting next to it, ready to tell the story yet again. "I cycled back from Dad's and I saw you out there doing a tour, so I put the kettle on. As I walked out to bring you the tea I got halfway across the yard and I could hear you going on a rant."

"Oh no, not the impression again!" laughed Mariella. But Rosie wasn't going to let her off that easily. She threw her hands onto her hips and stood up again to do a brilliant impersonation of her mum.

"It's Barney, actually. BARNEY. From DEVON. Not Greece. Not Spain. D-E-V-O-N."

Mariella threw down her fork and laughed hysterically.

"So then I remembered it was Friday and you needed rescuing more than the donkeys. I was deliberating whether to say there was a mouse or a rat. It took me about five presses on the microphone because I was cracking up. I had to

14

keep composing myself. And then finally I just held my nose – as you do for such customer announcements – and I swear I was mid-sentence when I thought, hang on, a rat is not bad enough. I mean, there actually *are* rats – I need something worse. And then it just came out. Cobra. I mean, what's worse than that?"

Mariella was now buckled up in stitches of laughter, with tears rolling down her cheek. "You are hilarious, Rosie. I think my favourite bit was how the mum took off like a cheetah. I never saw anything move so fast in my life. Didn't even grab her daughter's hand, just *whoooosh*."

Rosie was laughing hard and they continued to relive the scene, each time with the mum guessing the photo was taken in a different far-flung country and the dad conjuring up another random name for Barney the donkey. Rosie searched on Twitter to see if anyone had warned that a cobra was terrorising a Hampshire donkey sanctuary, but she found nothing, and they assumed the family had got home and realised they'd been tricked.

"Seriously, though," sighed Mariella, "people just don't care about the animals. They just want a nice little selfie for their social media, not a pic of an apparently 'tatty' donkey."

"Not everyone's like that, Mum. I mean, don't get me wrong, people love selfies – a lot. But most people care about animals too."

Mariella and Rosie walked towards the stable door, leaning their forks and brooms against the wall after a long day.

Chapter 3

Horse Sock World

Rosie came out of her bedroom yawning and gave her mum a kiss on the cheek. Mariella was at the dining table with her sewing machine, cloth spilling over onto the floor.

An enthusiastic estate agent might describe their home as 'cosy' and 'rustic', perhaps admitting it would 'benefit from some modernisation'. It had three bedrooms, a small kitchen and a living room with two sofas and a dining table. Wide pine floorboards ran throughout the house, blackened by years of farm life but softened by faded rugs. Wooden furniture – much of it hand crafted by

Mariella – was painted in sunny shades of orange, red and yellow.

It was always a mess because the last thing anyone wanted to do after a long day on the farm was clean the house. They preferred to eat off their laps than take on the monumental task of clearing the dining table. Even clearing off a chair might require rehoming a soldering iron, a scrunchie and a cat. Now and then Mariella and Rosie would blitz the house and take a bin liner of bric-a-brac to the tip, but inevitably they would come back with a carload of random objects to upcycle. "This saucepan would make a great pot for a cactus!" Rosie might say, while her mum loaded up a globe to convert into a lamp.

Rosie sleepily reached for a bowl from the cupboard. "What are you making?" she asked.

"Horse socks," replied Mariella, lifting up a long tube of material with black-and-white stripes going across the leg.

"Isn't it a bit hot for socks this time of year?" Rosie pondered as she shovelled Coco Pops into her mouth.

"It's for Lily. The flies are driving her nuts and apparently flies hate stripy colours, so this material is meant to help. You know what she's like, too –

she'll be showing them off all day long. As soon as there's a guest she's out there like a shot, trying to make friends."

Rosie nodded. The animals were like family members and each one had a unique personality.

"Mum, I did the accounts last night after we got in from the stables. It's not looking good."

Mariella replied jovially that it never looks good, but with a grave expression Rosie explained that this time was worse than normal. She sat down and pushed aside some material to make an enclave for her bowl, continuing:

"The thing is, there's nothing left to cut. We have to pay for the animal feed, the council tax, electricity and insurance. But there's nothing much left for the month of June. I'm afraid our monthly pay is going to be..."

"Wait! Drumroll please!" Mariella interrupted, grabbing two knitting needles from her sewing kit and tapping them on the table. She braced herself for the bad news, tensing as if waiting for an injection at the doctors.

"£54.12."

"Oh, that's all right! Phew!" she joked. "I thought you were going to say we only had something tiny like £53.23. I mean, 54 pounds AND twelve pence

– we're practically rich! Now, what do you think of this, Rosie?"

The horse socks she had created were so long that Mariella had to stand up to keep them from dangling onto the floor. Rosie said they looked brilliant (and they did) and teased her mum that she should sell them online to supplement her income. They joked that there must be an enormous market for horse socks and fantasised that eventually every self-respecting airport would have a sock shop for horses. They would call it "Horse Sock World" and their financial problems would be over.

They both knew that £54 in a month was not enough for their food shops, let alone clothes or anything else. The unspoken reality was that without cash they would eventually have to turn off the lights of Cranmore Donkey Sanctuary for good, and neither of them could bear the thought. Dad had already left, and they couldn't face losing their little piece of paradise too.

Rosie hesitated about having a second bowl of Coco Pops and put the twist-tie on, and Mariella said in a rare moment of seriousness:

"It's just so hard to run a tourist attraction. When I started this place ten years ago, it was for the animals, not because I thought people need yet another thing to entertain them. The animals have been hard work, for sure, but nothing like the stress caused by the people. Or lack of people. It feels like the last five years has been worrying about Tripadvisor reviews, collecting 'stars', posting 'stories'. It feels like every year I get further away from looking after animals and I become one of... *them*. Eventually we'll end up like Elvin McEadly and stop feeding the animals altogether."

Elvin McEadly was the owner of McZoo, a small wildlife park that bordered her property and topped the Tripadvisor list of "Things to do with kids in Westingbury" – an admittedly short list.

Rosie mulled over this for a moment. "Without the donkeys, there are no visitors. But it works the other way, too – without the visitors, there are no donkeys. Mum, think of it like this. When a car pulls up, don't think of it like a chore – 'Oh no, here comes another load of toddlers to trash the place.' A bale of straw is £10, so think of it like half a bale has arrived in the car park. More visitors mean more bales of straw for the long winter."

"That's if they even leave a donation at all, though. Most people don't even bother," her mum replied sadly, before lightening the mood. "Anyway, if you like customers so much, why are you frightening them off with talk of a cobra?" She ran over to tickle Rosie, who screamed and ran laughing out of the room. Mariella chased her down the hallway with her hands by her ears to make a cobra hood, hissing and poking her tongue out like a snake. Rosie shut herself in her bedroom and flopped onto her bed, laughing into her pillow.

Chapter 4

Goodbye Dad

"Don't worry," Mariella assured Rosie after school that day. "Summer holidays start tomorrow. I bet loads of visitors will come and maybe feel generous. Things will look up."

Rosie ate her beans and chips quietly that evening and remained unconvinced by her mum's eternal optimism. School holidays were better than term time, but even in August last year the sanctuary barely made any money. She walked her mum through income figures and the outgoings and showed that they would need about ten visitors every day, all summer, just to break even.

They often had one or two, and some days even none.

"If we need more donations, perhaps we should get more collection tubs made and put them around the local businesses. I know it's only a pound here and there, but if we had loads of them it might add up. We could put one at the fish 'n' chip place in Morley?" suggested Mariella, enthusiastically.

Rosie nodded and smiled. She agreed with what Dad had always said: that the time it took to drive around all the places to collect a few pounds would be better spent advertising to get more people through the gates.

Rosie knew better than to say, "Let's call Dad for a solution!" because her mum would give her the long speech about how her father was not interested in the hard work involved with running a place like this. The frustration Mariella had felt at coming in from the yard at sundown every night to find John on the sofa had driven a wedge into a previously joyful marriage. Still, it was almost Rosie's weekend to stay with her dad and she intended to consult him in secret.

John had moved out around a year ago, having resented the sanctuary and the pressure to work that came with it. He had never thought of himself as lazy and had been happy to help his beloved wife fulfil her dream of helping animals when they set up the business a decade ago. As time went on, the sanctuary began to consume every hour of their day, and eventually it consumed their marriage.

At first they loved being a young family and working hard together. Over time, John became exhausted and needed a better work–life balance. He wanted to see Mariella as his wife again and not just his business partner, and she agreed it sounded great. He set his hours as 8 AM till 5 PM, during which he cracked on with giving tours, doing accounts and running the social media pages. He tried to encourage his family to talk about different things over dinner so the sanctuary didn't envelop them. It would have been perfect, but Mariella could not switch off at 5 PM, or 6 PM... or ever. Her to-do list was overflowing, and as a natural grafter she always felt there was time to squeeze in one last job while she 'had the light'. When she finally came in and heated up her tea, she would watch with jealousy as Rosie and John laughed over a game of *Quizamid*.

John resented feeling guilty for finishing work at 5 PM like everyone else he knew, and the friction became too much. With he and Mariella going for weeks at a time without even eating a meal together, the day he packed his bags and left did not come as a shock to anyone.

Rosie was eleven at the time and mature enough to feel relief at the thought of the tension dissipating. She was glad her dad had found a little house to rent just a ten-minute walk away from hers, and she knew in her heart that one day her mum and dad's love for each other would bring them back together.

"I'm only going round the corner. I love you, Mariella," he had said as he tearfully left, hugging his wife of eight years at the door. "I wish we could do this, but we can't. There's just not enough hours in the day for this place and us." Mariella had held Rosie tightly as Dad walked out of the car park for the final time.

Chapter 5

Tandem

It was Thursday afternoon when Rosie bounded across the car park in her school uniform, vaulted the gate and sprinted across the yard to the house. School had finally finished for the term and the summer holidays had begun. She threw her uniform in the wash and put on some shorts, wellies and a top, which would become her new uniform for the next six weeks.

Rosie quite liked school, but she wouldn't miss it in the summer. She found the lessons interesting, loving computers, maths and especially science. She had decided back in primary school she would like to become a vet eventually and constantly amazed her teachers with her technical and practical knowledge. Last week they had been learning to label the parts of a flowering plant, which was a breeze for Rosie who had been growing fruit and vegetables in her own section of the greenhouse since she was seven. She had long understood the difference between growing from seed or cutting, and how to artificially pollinate using a tiny paintbrush in the absence of bees. Still, she was not one to show off and just quietly got on with labelling the diagram before the teacher had even finished handing out the worksheets. The only part of school she didn't like was lunchtime. She had one good friend called Hannah, but her bestie was her mum, so she always wished she could work through lunch and go home an hour early instead.

Rosie stood out in the yard in the hot sun, holding her hands over her eyes.

"Can I look yet?" she shouted through the double doors of her mum's workshop.

"Almost!" called Mariella, before finally saying, "Okay, you can look now."

Rosie uncovered her eyes and saw a tandem bicycle. She inspected it lovingly, walking around it and drinking in every detail. The metal wheels and handlebars had been polished and gleamed in the sun. It had mismatched everything – the front tyre was skinny and the one on the back was from a mountain bike. The front saddle was plastic and the back one – which she assumed, correctly, was hers – was leather. The frame was painted in a dark blue shade she recognised immediately as the protective paint that they used each year to coat the troughs. The front had a big wooden crate that fitted into a strong frame that had been welded to the handlebars, and behind the back saddle was another homemade metal framework with a bag each side.

"Mum, it's BEAUTIFUL! I love it. Did you make this? Well, obviously!"

"Aw, glad you like it. I had to sell the car, so we needed a way of getting around for the summer. It's only temporary. I'll get a new one when we have a bit more money coming in. I found this frame and all the parts at the tip, and I've been working on it for a month. Anyway, who needs a car?" Mariella continued. "They're bad for the environment, and in this thing we can most definitely carry a weekly shop."

"Mum, I think you might be overestimating how much food we can buy with our £14!" Rosie teased, eagerly jumping on so they could give it a spin around the yard.

Chapter 6

Rosie's Model

Over that first weekend of the holidays, a trickle of visitors came in, but as Rosie had expected it was a poor turnout and nowhere near enough to begin catching up on their monthly bank payments.

Rosie spent the weekend with her dad at his kitchen table giving life to an idea she had been chewing over in her mind for some months. With a combination of computer spreadsheets and old-fashioned glue and cardboard, she was building the future of Cranmore Donkey Sanctuary. On Sunday afternoon she carefully picked up her work and walked it back to her house to show her mum.

"It's amazing, Rosie," said Mariella as she circled the dining table, marvelling at the structure in front of her. "What is it?"

"It's Cranmore Donkey Sanctuary 2.0," Rosie explained. "I wanted to surprise you with it. I've had this idea for a while, that if we borrow some money from the bank we could upgrade this park and hopefully turn things around."

The model was based on a sheet of cardboard that took up most of the table. It was snow white like a proper architectural model, with a scattering of neat little buildings made of old birthday cards. Connecting up the buildings were raised roads and paths cut out of cardboard. Tiny white fences and walls completed the model, and perched in the pastures were trees made of wire and cotton wool, and some cutouts of animals.

"Don't you recognise it, Mum? Look, there's our car park, which I've extended because it'd be great to be able to have twenty cars in it at once for busy weekends. There's the entrance and the ticket office, which remains mostly the same as our Portakabin we have now except I've cut a hole out here to sell tickets without needing people to come right in. Yes, you heard me right – selling tickets, rather than asking politely for donations. This little building here houses the toilets, including disabled access ramp, because our portaloos won't cut it when we have twenty families at one time! The stables are in the same place, but by making one big new building instead of all the existing ones huddled together, we've got room for 35 animals, not just sixteen. And they all have access to the paddock without always having to walk them through the yard. And wait..."

Rosie reached over and turned off the lights, before flicking a switch on the model. It lit up with fairy lights on sticks. Mariella gasped with joy and clapped her hands together, and Rosie continued her virtual tour.

"...And it has floodlights so that the whole park can stay open till 6 PM all year round so we can still do after school, even in the winter. So, what do you think, Mum?"

A tear rolled down Mariella's cheek as she beamed with pride at what her daughter had created.

"It's gorgeous, Rosie. So gorgeous. Like you. That must have taken you ages! I can't believe how well you thought it out."

"Dad helped me. It was really fun to build. I have been wanting to do this project with you, but also wanted to surprise you, so I just did it. It'd cost a lot of money to build and we'd need planning permission apparently. Dad helped me write a list of everything we'd need to buy, and how much it would cost."

Mariella was stunned at her daughter's ingenuity, poring over her calculations in the spreadsheet.

"Rosie, I can't believe you did this. I actually can't believe your dad helped you design something that makes the park even bigger, too! That's so sweet of him, knowing he'd probably take a bulldozer to it if it was up to him. Wow. When I think back to when I was twelve, the idea that I could understand all this stuff like 'profit' and 'planning permission' – I mean, I'm 38 and I'm still clueless!"

The two of them laughed, and Mariella said she would book a meeting with Peter, their bank manager, first thing in the morning. She wanted to convince him to lend them the money to enact Rosie's marvellous plan.

Chapter 7

The Bank

At 9 AM when it opened, Mariella got on the phone to the local bank in their nearby town of Westingbury. Their bank manager was surprised to hear from them and said he'd been meaning to call her and would see them that very afternoon. Mariella asked if there was any chance he could come to them, since they had something they wanted to show him that would have been impossible to transport even on their tandem. He was happy for an excuse to get out of the office on this hot summer's day.

"So, Mum, I can look after the ticket office while you talk to Peter. I figure it's not a good look to be closing the park on the day we're asking for a loan!"

Mariella replied, "Are you kidding me? As if I'm going to pitch this without you! It's your idea, Rosie. You *have* to be in that meeting."

"I'd love to, but then who is going to look after the front gate? Shall I call Dad?" offered Rosie.

"It's okay, I've got it all sorted. I called Cass and she's coming. Her college has broken up for the summer so she is happy for some work."

Rosie simply said, "O. M. G!", and her mum laughed.

Cass was seventeen years old and lived in a tranquil village just the other side of Westingbury. She had learned to ride a horse while most kids her age were on balance bikes. At ten she was entering equine events around the county and her room began to fill with trophies. She started to work at the donkey sanctuary on Saturdays at age fourteen, around the time she evolved into "Badass Cass". You could hear her coming as if a festival were in town, because she had her headphones blaring out punk rock, worn around her neck instead of actually on her ears. Her hair colour changed on a weekly basis, and she wore a leather jacket with 'Ramones' painted on it, her favourite band. The riding trophies were now boxed up in the loft and her new passion was 'mixed media artwork', which she studied at the college in Westingbury. Her creations were wild and brilliant.

Rosie and her dad had visited her last exhibition, which ingeniously showed the two parts of her life – horses and punk rock – through an installation where smashed-up records hung on wires from the ceiling at eye level. As you walked around the sculpture it seemed like just a messy chandelier of shards of plastic, and most of the parents and visitors dismissed it as a bit of a mess. But those who spent a few more minutes circling the artwork were rewarded by the realisation that when you stood at a certain spot on the floor, all the plastic pieces lined up perfectly to show the shape of a beautiful black horse.

Around lunchtime, they heard a car cough and choke its way into the car park, and Cass came in, beaming.

"All right, Pandaface!" she yelled at Rosie, who chuckled and remembered that Cass had, for years now, never called her the same thing twice.

They hugged and Rosie showed Cass the model she had made. Naturally, this was right up her street as an artist, and she was incredibly proud of Rosie, who she doted on like a sister.

A more sombre moment was when their bank manager Peter arrived at 2 PM. His hair was greying and his face was always red. Mariella had originally thought he was always puffed out from being a little overweight, but she realised over the years that his face was red because of his penchant for red wine with lunch, at dinner and occasionally at his desk. Every time they saw him he looked more like his drink. He wore a waistcoat that hung loosely on his large frame, and he mopped his brow with a handkerchief as he sweated his way to the ticket booth. He seemed flustered and anxious as Mariella ushered him into the office and made tea.

"As I said, Mariella, I've been meaning to call you. There's some important business we need to take care of."

She cut him off and sat down at the table with the model on it. "Before you continue, Peter, let me say it for you. We're always late with our payments, and we're sorry. We do appreciate all that the bank has done for us and we do take our bills seriously. In fact, that's what we wanted to show you."

Peter tried to interject, but he couldn't get a word in edgeways as Mariella continued her speech. He shook slightly as he lifted his cup of tea to his lips.

"So, as you know, it's always been tough to make our business profitable, especially with McZoo right around the corner. We believe we have a solution though, which we present right here. This is a model of what our sanctuary could become if we can get a small additional loan."

She talked him through the model – the enlarged car park, new toilets, and so on – as Rosie had done the previous evening. Peter nodded politely and nervously sipped his tea. Finally, when she was done, she said, "What do you think?"

He set his tea down and cleared his throat, loosening his collar a little in the heat of the portakabin.

"Mariella, I appreciate the time you've taken to create this model. I really do. I like the, er... horse things. Further lending is not going to be an option from us, I'm afraid, and I have some bad news. As you know, Knightwood Bank bought this land ten years ago."

"Well, you mean *we* bought this land with money we borrowed from you," Mariella tried to correct him, with a confused look on her face.

"No, Mariella, the Knightwood Bank owns this land, and you make payments towards it monthly. As you may recall many moons ago, the bank bought Ciderwood Farm, as it was originally known, and you make rental payments monthly. After twenty years – or sooner if you paid back the whole amount it cost us – *then* you would own the land outright and the deal is done. But right now, this land still belongs to us."

Mariella's face began to feel warm, her throat went dry and she felt sick with stress. She hated the money side of the business at the best of times, and this conversation was heading in a particularly sinister direction. Rosie listened intently and held her mother's hand.

Peter continued, somewhat robotically as if he had rehearsed his speech.

"So you need to remember that this property belongs to us, and we have to do what's in the interest of the bank. As you know, you have been late in making payments for the last few years and it has been agreed at the bank – and I hasten to add this is not my decision, Mariella, it has been taken at a higher level at corporate headquarters – that the bank must now sell the property."

"Wait; what? You're selling our farm? But this is our business, our livelihood. That right there is our house. Where do you expect us to go?" Tears streamed down Mariella's cheeks, and she gripped her daughter's hand tightly. "You can't take our farm away from us! We've been paying you rent for ten years. Yes, we've been late once or twice, but that isn't a reason to take away our life! And what about the animals? Where do you think they're going to go?"

Peter put an A4-sized envelope on the model and closed up his briefcase, eager to escape what had become one of the most uncomfortable meetings of his life.

"I'm sorry, Mariella, that it has come to this. I'm afraid the business has not been as successful as it was initially forecast, and the bank has to deploy its resources in the most efficient way. You have six weeks' notice, as per the original contract, and then the bank will be selling the land. Look, I want to help you, but I can't make exceptions based on individuals or it wouldn't be fair."

"Not fair? NOT FAIR?" she screamed. "I'll tell you what's not fair. Walking into our farm and telling us we've got six weeks to pack up sixteen animals and our entire lives and be homeless. That's what's not fair! Get out. NOW!"

Mariella leapt to her feet and swatted Peter with the envelope he had left at the table. As he jumped up from his chair and turned to the door, he lost his balance and began to topple over. Mariella noticed he had strange shoes on with little rubber spikes underneath, which had caught in the flooring. In what seemed like slow motion, he came crashing down like a great oak being felled, plunging onto the table and smashing the model to pieces. Mariella and Rosie's jaws fell open as he scrambled back to his feet and waddled his way out of the door and down the steps. As he got halfway towards his car, he heard a voice say:

"Peter, I have a question."

He paused and turned around, surprised to hear from Rosie, who had not yet spoken a word since he had arrived.

"How much is left on the loan? I mean, you said we own it when we pay back the full amount. So how much would we need to pay now to finish up the loan and own the farm?"

"Well, you have £40,000 remaining." He was flustered and humiliated by his fall. Desperate to get to the safety of his car, his true lack of empathy was now evident. "Yes, I suppose you are right, Rosie. If you've got £40,000 in one of those sheds then you can buy it outright. You'd better get looking, though, because like I say, you've got six weeks from the date on the letter. You need to be gone by then."

With that, he jogged towards his car and exited the car park in a cloud of dust.

Chapter 8

Six Weeks to Go

Peter's visit marked the darkest day in the history of Cranmore Donkey Sanctuary. There had been sad times before when they had had to say goodbye to animals, and particularly when John had left, but none of them compared to the day they discovered they would lose their farm altogether. There was no silver lining or bright side to look on, just an enormous to-do list associated with tearing down everything they had built and having to start over.

After the meeting, Mariella hugged Rosie and they both cried. Cass put on a brave face and shielded customers from the two of them sobbing in the office, while she kept the park open for the rest of the afternoon.

Mariella took time to go through the original contract, and unfortunately Peter was right about the situation. She explained to a tearful Rosie. "I've been reading it line by line just now, and it does look like the bank is within its rights to sell it. I am ashamed to say I never fully understood it till now, but you have to remember it was ten years ago when I signed that thing along with your dad, and at the time we were just so delighted to be able to buy the farm we would have signed anything. The monthly payments seemed achievable – we didn't realise how hard it would be to keep up. We never realised – or maybe just never imagined it would happen – that if we got late with payments then the bank could sell the place and boot us out. So Peter's right that they can give us six weeks to leave. We will be given the £60,000 that we've put into this place over the last ten years, which is something, but land prices have gone up so much that it's not like we can buy another farm with it. It could be a deposit on a house, I suppose, but never again would a bank lend us the money to

45

buy a farm if we couldn't keep the first one. It would still mean saying goodbye to this place."

That evening, Mariella was out sweeping the yard with Rosie. She knew that she should put down the broom and write a list of everything that needed doing. She recalled friends at other sanctuaries she might contact to start the process of rehoming her animals. She should start looking for jobs in the real world and find a new house to rent for her and Rosie. It was too early to face all that, though, and she just wanted to sweep. Some people have yoga or meditation, and for Mariella it was hard graft. Nothing would clear her mind like a mundane and repetitive task.

Rosie came and joined her in the yard as the sun was starting to lower over the fields.

"Dinner's nearly ready," her daughter smiled.

"Wait," said Mariella. "Aren't I meant to be the one calling *you* in for dinner? Ha ha. What are we having?"

"Fish finger sandwiches."

"My absolute favourite! You're the best, Rosie. I'm amazed we have bread."

"I went round to get some from Dad's," Rosie confessed.

Mariella leaned her broom against the stable door and stroked the face of one of her favourite donkeys, Bella. She found comfort in her warm grey fur. She knew she would miss the donkeys terribly.

Mariella walked towards the house and was joined by her daughter.

"So, I take it you told Dad about the bank? I suppose in some ways he probably wishes it had happened years ago so we could have gone back to the normal nine-to-five life he always wanted."

"He was so sad for us. Said he'd do anything he could to help. He said we could stay at his place while we get back on our feet... if we want?" Rosie said hopefully, and her mum gave a non-committal nod.

They ate their fish finger sandwiches and Mariella washed up.

"Rosie, I know it's getting dark and all of this seems a bit pointless now, but do you want to go and clean out Bella's stall with me? If I sit around this house I'll just get emotional. Everywhere I look there's a picture that'll have to go into a box, or another reminder of something that'll be gone forever. I think I just need to stay busy today."

47

Rosie felt the same, and they both pulled on their wellies and headed back out into the dusky evening, picking up their pitchforks and brooms. As they chatted, they began to wrap their heads around how there could be life after this. Mariella talked about the practicalities of closing down in six weeks as she sat down on a bale of hay. She would need to look for a job, find a house to rent and rehome many animals.

"It's like anything, I suppose. It seems impossible, but we just have to break it down into small sections and work through it. I'll write a list tomorrow and we'll get through it one by one till it's all sold or packed up or gone."

The two of them forced a smile and went to bed after what had been the longest and toughest day in the history of Cranmore Donkey Sanctuary.

Chapter 9

A Generous Offer

The next day, a tired old Jaguar pulled up at Cranmore Donkey Sanctuary. It seemed like a fancy car to Mariella. It was a Tuesday, and Rosie was out and about in the yard explaining the difference between a donkey and a mule to a family with young children. Out of the car stepped a tall, bony man dressed in tartan golfing trousers, a tweed jacket and a peaked cap. He made his way to the door and poked his head in.

"Ms Harpel, I presume? It is delightful to meet you at last. I have heard wonderful things. I am Elvin McEadly, from the world-famous McZoo."

He curtseyed theatrically and invited himself into the Portakabin. He placed a box of chocolates on the table, which Mariella later discovered were two years past their 'best before' date.

"Oh, right. It's nice to meet you after all these years," said Mariella, taken aback at the unexpected visitor. "I have also heard... things. You can call me Mariella, and thanks for the chocolates. So, Elvin, what can I do for you?"

"Shall we walk and talk?" he asked. Mariella followed him outside and locked the office door shut.

He began, "It's a lovely facility you have here. I don't consider you a competitor – because after all, we do very different things – but I'm sure we share some of the same difficulties in keeping up visitor numbers and paying the food bills. Now, you have a wonderfully large plot here. What is it? Fifteen acres?"

"It's 25 acres," Mariella replied.

"Ooh, is it? That's more than I thought. So you have 25 acres, and it butts right up to my zoo over on that boundary, if I'm correct."

Mariella led the way through the yard and opened a gate, inviting Elvin into one of the paddocks.

"Yes." She motioned. "From that feeding trough to the blue gate there, we border your zoo. We're close enough that our donkeys have learned to ignore the roar of your lion, put it that way."

"Yes. How wonderful. Good old Leo. As I say, I know how difficult it can be to run a leisure attraction in this market, and how expensive it can be. Let me cut to the chase. I have plenty of room and would be interested in taking on some of your animals. You know, if you found yourself in a position to no longer be able to look after them here, for example. I say that as one conservationist to another."

Mariella was surprised at his offer, since she had only ever heard bad things about Elvin. So much so that in the ten years she had run Cranmore Donkey Sanctuary she had never once gone to introduce herself to him. Word was that he didn't care about animals at all and saw his zoo as a money-making machine. Rob – a friend of Cass who worked occasionally at the donkey sanctuary – had noticed Elvin routinely parking in the disabled spot in Westingbury Town Centre. Still, this was a generous offer, considering donkeys need a lot of space and don't exactly draw the crowds.

While Elvin took a phone call in his car, Mariella explained his proposal to Rosie. With Peter's six-week deadline front of mind, the two of them reluctantly agreed that it made sense to begin rehoming their donkeys with their wealthy neighbour. She and Rosie agreed to send Esther, an older donkey who had been with them for three years, and figured that if all went well then they would consider sending more across at a later date. Arrangements were made and Mariella thanked Elvin for taking the initiative and coming round to introduce himself.

Over the rest of that Tuesday, Rosie sadly packed up Esther's bits and pieces into a cardboard box. She cried that night as she went to sleep, trying to stay quiet so she would not wake her mum in the next-door room. The idea of losing the farm had felt unbelievable till now: just words and financial arrangements she did not fully understand. Packing up Esther's collar, rope and favourite food bowl had brought home how painful this process was going to be. First she had watched Dad leave; now it would be the animals, and in just a few weeks it would be her and Mum walking through the gates for the last time.

The following day, a young man in a McZoo shirt drove Esther out of the gates of Cranmore Donkey Sanctuary in a horse box. Mariella put her arm around Rosie as they watched them leave.

Mariella felt relieved to have met someone else locally who did really care about animals, and also ashamed to have taken on more than she could manage. After all, lack of money was the very reason that most of these donkeys had been rehomed with her in the first place. She thought about how she must get used to this sad moment of seeing them being carted away. She and Rosie consoled themselves with the fact that Esther would be nearby and they could go and visit her easily.

On Thursday, they locked up the visitor centre early and got on the tandem to visit Esther at McZoo. They were excited to see her settled into her deluxe living quarters. Riding the tandem was a strange feeling for Rosie, who wasn't used to pedalling a bike whilst not being able to steer. The two of them soon found they could synchronise their pedalling, and they loved being able to chat to each other as they cycled around the lanes towards the gates of McZoo.

Mariella speculated that Esther probably had her own sign on the door, to which Rosie said, "I bet she has a sign with lights around it like a pop star's dressing room."

"And of course, a huge mirror for doing her make-up and a wardrobe so she can choose which donkey jacket she'll wear today," Mariella added.

"*She* chooses? Surely you're referring to her assistant!"

And so it went on, till by the time they arrived they were certain Esther would by now have her own castle, guarded by the lion himself.

How wrong they were.

Chapter 10

Where is Esther?

Mariella and Rosie locked up the tandem in front of the zoo, joking that if someone stole it they might have a hard time selling it. A blue tandem with mismatched saddles and enormous carrying capacity might be a bit conspicuous.

McZoo was significantly more substantial than their donkey sanctuary. The car park was several times larger and the entrance had turnstiles and a ticket booth at which they had to explain they had come to see Elvin McEadly. They were ushered through and given directions to an office building where he worked. Before they went to see him, they decided to explore and find Esther for themselves.

The zoo consisted of a doughnut-shaped road that might take 30 minutes to walk around if you didn't stop to check out the animals. It was much bigger than their donkey sanctuary and had a cafe and gift shop. The whole place looked tired and neglected. Paint flaked off the signposts and weeds grew from cracks in the pavement.

There was a penguin enclosure, a reptile house, an aviary, some lemurs and the all-important lion. Rosie instantly recognised the penguins as Humboldt penguins and she and her mum chatted about how odd it is that the word 'penguin' comes from Welsh ('white head'), despite there being no wild penguins in Wales. Their water looked murky and green, and Rosie wondered whether she would be a happier penguin if she were huddled in the freezing Antarctic or stuck in this small enclosure.

The aviary was small and they moved through it quickly, feeling sorry for the birds, which couldn't fly around far. The flamingos in the field next door had plenty of space, although their wings were clipped to prevent them flying home to Africa. The thought made Mariella and Rosie sadder still, and they worried that Esther's accommodation might be cramped.

Next was the reptile house containing a small Burmese Python. Rosie had seen a documentary about how these snakes were causing havoc in Florida, where they had become an invasive species. Many pet snakes had escaped from their homes when a hurricane tore through Florida in the 1990s. The snakes had slithered into the swampland and were now flourishing.

It was late in the day and only a few visitors were still at the zoo. Mariella observed with interest their fascination with the snake, despite the fact that the animal didn't move a millimetre the whole time they were staring at it. She thought about how hard it was to get people to take an interest in her donkeys by comparison.

Finally, they reached the lion enclosure. The sign read:

> *Species: Lion*
> *From: Africa*
> *Diet: Meat*

Rosie laughed and said it was a bit worrying they didn't know where in Africa it was from, or what exactly it ate. Its enclosure was small and it paced round and round, looking quite depressed.

They had now completed the entire lap of the park and there was no sign of Esther, so they asked at the office, which was closing up. The receptionist was visibly annoyed at a guest delaying his exit from the park.

"We don't offer refunds, just to let you know. Our policy is on the wall there."

Mariella said, "Actually, we couldn't find our donkey, so we wanted to ask Elvin McEadly where her new enclosure is."

"I believe Elvin's at golf this afternoon. Let me just look at his calendar."

Up on the wall in the office was a colour-coded calendar. On almost every cell was written the word 'Golf' in green pen. Literally golf in the morning and golf in the afternoon.

"He plays a lot of golf, as you can see," said the McZoo employee with a vacant smile.

The conversation was interrupted by the phone ringing, and he answered it. "McZoo; how can I help you? ... Yes, that's fine, let me put it on the calendar. So that's 40 kg coming next Monday – the 27th. Yes, I think we have enough till then."

He hung up the phone and Mariella continued. "As I was saying, we came here..."

"Just a minute please. Let me get this marked," he said, standing to write on the calendar in blue pen: *40 kg meat delivery*.

"Oh, silly me," he chastised himself as he crossed it out and rewrote it in red.

"Okay, so you came here to see Elvin? I'm afraid he's at golf. Perhaps you could try his mobile. Now if there's nothing else?" He rudely stood up and herded them towards and out of the door.

Mariella tried Elvin's phone, but it went to voicemail, so the two of them headed home.

That evening at dinner, they discussed where Esther might be.

"I wonder if he's keeping her at another facility, ready for her big debut. I think she'll be there tomorrow anyway," said Mariella.

"How do you mean, Mum?"

"Oh, on the calendar with golf all over it, it said 'Donkey' starting tomorrow and a long red arrow filling up the whole week. I figure she's the main event, you know – a focus for their marketing for a week or so. The big launch."

Rosie's eyes widened and she gulped her mouthful of food down. "Mum, that's not good! Did you say it was written in red? That's the colour he used to write down the meat delivery."

Mariella was confused. "What do you mean? You can't give meat to a donkey."

"No," said Rosie, "but you can give a donkey to a lion. What if Esther is going to tide them over till this 40 kg meat delivery?"

Mariella set her knife and fork down as the gravity of the situation hit her. "Oh my goodness, 'Donkey' was marked on for tomorrow. We've got to go back and find her! Heaven forbid he feeds her to the lion before we can stop him!"

It was around 8 PM when the two realised Esther needed to be rescued – if indeed it wasn't already too late for that. They thought about leaving it till first thing in the morning and being there when the zoo opened, but they knew they would be worried all night. McZoo was only the other side of the fence from their own land, so they decided they must climb the fence and try to find Esther again, right now.

Chapter 11

The Great Donkey Rescue

At dusk, the two of them set off from their bungalow across the yard and onto the fields. Mariella had grabbed some bolt cutters and a few tools in case they needed to open up a padlock or cut through a fence. Rosie was feeling optimistic about finding Esther and brought a rope to lead her home. They convinced themselves that if Elvin really was planning to feed her to a lion, she would take a lot of room in a freezer. Surely it would make sense for McZoo to keep her alive till feeding time came, they reasoned. The thought made their stomachs turn.

Mariella and Rosie were not fans of the colour black, so it was difficult for them to dress for a daring raid. Mariella had recovered one of John's black t-shirts from her workshop, where she had been using it as an oily rag. She wore denim shorts, as always, but had covered her legs with a pair of Lily's horse socks, hoping the zebra pattern would break up her outline. Rosie burst out laughing when she saw her mum, but she looked just as ridiculous in a pair of navy-blue pyjamas with silver unicorns on, the only dark clothing she could find in her wardrobe.

Wearing head torches, they weaved their way through the dense bushes where their property bordered McZoo. There was a chain-link fence about head height, and they helped each other to climb over it near a post. Finally they found themselves in a small copse of trees inside the awful zoo they had grown to despise. Mariella whispered to Rosie to turn off her headlamp so nobody would spot them, and continued:

"Rosie, whatever we do, we must not wake up that lion. You can hear it roar for miles and it'll be like a burglar alarm going off."

Rosie nodded, and they gingerly crept out from the shadows to get their bearings. The ground beneath their feet was grass and they realised at once they were inside the flamingo enclosure, surrounded by birds sleeping peacefully on one leg. Quiet as mice, the pair tiptoed past the birds towards the fence, which they climbed over to reach the road that circled around the park.

The first building to search was between the aviary and the flamingos, and Mariella lifted Rosie up to peek through its window. She looked down at her mum and shook her head. The hoot of an owl made them jump, and they scrambled into the shadows at the side of the shed.

As Mariella inched towards the next building, Rosie grabbed her t-shirt and pulled her back, pointing up at a security camera staring down at the road ahead of them. They would have to go the other way. They headed for another building a little further along the road towards the penguin enclosure.

They shone their torches into the windows of the many sheds and buildings, but all they found were tools and animal feed. Rosie had to sit on her mum's shoulders to peek into the windows of one, but again they found nothing alive.

They had crept around the zoo for about twenty minutes and there remained just one more, large building to search. Unfortunately it was perilously close to the main office, which had a light on. Still, they had no choice but to edge towards it, aided by the moonlight.

This building was more like a barn or warehouse, with wavy metal sides reaching up to the height of a house. As they crossed the road to get to it, the office door opened and they saw a patch of light spill out onto the path in front of it. Mariella and Rosie darted behind the corner of the warehouse building and watched a huge security guard emerge with a torch in one hand and a pasty in the other. He stood in the doorway of the office, blocking its light entirely as he shone his torch out into the darkness.

"It's an eclipse!" whispered Rosie, but her mum was too nervous to laugh.

Rotating slowly like a lighthouse, the great brick of a man shone his beam from left to right. As it came towards their hiding place, they dived back behind the wall of the warehouse and lay flat on the ground. They heard gravel crunch as the great ogre walked out of his cave. Thankfully, the sounds got quieter, and they realised he had set off up the road away from their hiding place.

"This is our chance!" whispered Mariella as she left the cover of the warehouse and went towards the doorway. It had a pair of metal sliding doors, tall and wide enough to drive a truck through, shut with a padlock as big as a fist.

"We'll never get through it with my bolt cutters – it's too thick," Mariella said.

Rosie peered up the road that the security guard had taken. Then she sprang across the gravel and up the steps into the main office he had just vacated! Mariella wanted to shout after her to stop, but she knew she must stay silent and trust her daughter.

A few minutes passed – although it felt to Mariella like hours – before Rosie leapt down the steps of the office and ran back across the gravel area to her mum. In her hand she had a key whose tag read 'Main Barn'.

They tried the key in the lock. It pinged open, and the two ninjas slid the door open just enough to slip inside.

With their torches on, they were able to see that the huge barn was full of farm machinery: tractors, a digger and equipment for spraying pesticides.

Then they saw that at the back was a set of wooden stalls for livestock. Mariella ran to it, and there was Esther, lying on the concrete floor of one of the stalls, with not even a bed of straw or any water to drink. She looked weak and tired, but she recognised Rosie and staggered to her feet, braying excitedly.

"Shhhh, Esty," Rosie said, rubbing her face kindly. "Let's get you out of here!"

With Esther on a length of rope held by Rosie, they carefully made their way through the building and out of the doors. They spotted a pool of light moving on the road in the distance and knew it must be the guard making his way back to the main office. He was now talking on his mobile phone, and to avoid being spotted, the trio hid behind the warehouse building in the same spot they had used before. They were so close they could hear his conversation, and they were desperate to make sure Esther did not make any noise to alert him.

"As I've said, boss," he barked, "I've done a full lap of the premises and there's nothing open and nothing to note. I'm not sure what the noises were but I think it must be a false alarm… Again? Yes, okay, I'll do another lap, boss. Leave it with me."

With that, the guard put his phone in his pocket and let out an audible sigh, before setting off once more up the road.

Mariella whispered to Rosie, "Now, remember this place has one long road that loops in a big circle. We're at the bottom of that circle now, and we need to get to the top because that's where the fence connects to our farm. Let's race up the opposite way as fast as we can and get to the top before he does."

"But Mum, look how weak Esther is. She doesn't look like she's been fed since they took her, and I don't think she'll be able to run today. I know this sounds crazy, but how about we *follow* the security guard up this way? We know he's doing a full loop – he did before – so as long as we stay a long way behind him, we can't get busted."

With that as the agreed plan, the three of them checked that the guard was long gone and followed behind him, trying as best they could to remain in the shadows to the side of the road. At times they could hear him in the distance, rattling cages and talking to himself, venting at having to walk around while his other pasties got cold.

Finally they reached the trees where they had climbed the fence earlier. Mariella whipped the bolt cutters from her backpack and snipped through the metal wire fence, yanking it from each side to make a hole big enough for Esther to get through. As soon as they got to the other side, they twisted it shut as best they could and high-fived each other at having successfully completed their heist. Rosie untied Esther, who eagerly trotted to a trough where she gulped down some water and set to work on the grass.

"Mum, that was brilliant! Breaking into a zoo and stealing a donkey! Well, 'reclaiming', not stealing. And your outfit! I mean, does it get better than that?"

They were ecstatic at having managed to rescue her before it was too late, but Mariella's happiness soon evolved into anger at how Elvin McEadly had brazenly turned up at her sanctuary and tricked her into giving him an animal, knowing full well he intended to use it as lion food.

This meant war.

Chapter 12

Brainstorm

Rosie awoke to hear a kind of scratching noise, and she wondered what was going on. She sleepily put on her slippers and shuffled through to the kitchen, where she saw her mum standing on a stool and drawing on the cupboard doors.

"Oh, hey lovely!" Mariella said with a sparkle in her eye. She rushed over and hugged Rosie. "You were right, of course, Rosie, that day you asked Peter about the remaining money! Are we really going to pack all our stuff into boxes and roll over like a dead duck? Let those awful pinstripe money-hoarders take our farm without even putting up a fight? Feed our donkeys to a lion? No! We just have to play by their rules. Money, money, money. That's the name of the game. We had six weeks, right? We wasted half a week moping around, but we still have five and a half weeks. That's 40 days to make £40,000. So let's figure out how we get £1,000 *today*."

Rosie smiled and hugged her mum. It was so wonderful to see her wild, determined soul rush back into the outline of a person who had been in despair for the last few days.

"Okay, now we're talking. But why are you drawing all over the cupboards? What are you, five? I feel like I should tell you off!" joked Rosie.

Mariella looked at what she'd drawn, almost surprising herself. "Oh, well, we don't have a whiteboard."

She glanced at the pen in her hand and read the word 'Permanent Marker' on the side.

"Or a whiteboard marker. Well... if we fail, they'll tear this place down, then nobody will care about the kitchen cupboards. But if we *win*, Rosie..."

Mariella strode towards her dramatically, with a marker pen in her hand and a glint of insanity in her eyes, cupping Rosie's cheeks in her hands.

"If we *win*, then will we really care that we ruined the kitchen cupboards? No way! We'll love it! We'll look at them every time we get a tin of beans out and say, 'Ah yes, that time we fought the bank and won. That summer we plucked forty THOUSAND pounds out of thin air."

After whirling around the kitchen and laughing, her mum's tone snapped back to reality.

"Okay, grab a pen, Rosie. I have no idea how we're going to do this. So far I've got the idea of selling fish finger sandwiches and pasties. And by the way, we only have those on the menu because I had tried to write 'Pastries' and missed out an R. Then I thought, hmm, pasties. Probably sell for more than pastries. See, that's how ruthless the new Mariella is! Mwah ha ha!"

The two of them laughed loudly and Rosie picked up a pen, adding to the spider diagram that exploded into life across several white cupboards. Out from the word 'Marketing' sprang lines towards 'Facebook', 'Instagram' and 'TripAdvisor'. From 'Tripadvisor' came yet more lines leading to 'Get 5 stars' and 'Beat McZoo'; and so it went on.

They had started so early that by the time they slumped back into their dining chairs to marvel at their work, it was only just after 8 AM. Curiously, there was a knock at the door, and Mariella opened it in her pyjamas. It was Cass, who came armed with her lunch in a paper bag.

"Oh, hi, Cass, you're up early. I didn't know you were working with us today."

"Hi, Mariella. Hi, Badgernose!" she shouted back into the kitchen, inviting herself into the house. She kicked off her Dr Martens at the door, waltzed in and sat down with the others.

"Yeah, well I quit my job at the call centre and didn't have a lot on my plate. So I thought I'd come and work here for the summer. For free, mind. I know you've somehow got even less than no money. I either sit around all summer at home or come and work, and I'd rather be here and actually doing something to help. That is helpful, right?"

Mariella was touched by her generosity and thanked her. "Are you sure, Cass? That's huge."

"Defo, Mrs H. You guys are like my second family. There's nowhere I'd rather be," Cass assured her.

Mariella excused herself to take a shower, and Rosie told Cass the story of their heist the previous evening. At 9 AM the three of them pulled on their boots and headed out into the yard to prepare for opening at ten. Mariella and Rosie planned to head out on the tandem and pick up food supplies from Cranmore village.

"I liked your diagram on the kitchen cupboards," said Cass. "It's funny you wrote 'Instagram' – did I tell you about the zebra legs yesterday?"

"No, what's that about?" said Mariella.

"You guys were heading to McZoo – first time – and I was giving the tour to some people. It wasn't your usual family with little kids, it was two guys and two girls about my age. I left them to it and they were going round stroking the animals, and then I noticed from a distance they're posing by Lily and taking photos, but basically pointing their camera at the ground. Weird. I know a thing or two about photography and wanted to help them, so I go over and offer to take their picture for them. I raise it up to get the whole of Lily and they're like, 'No, actually we wanted to frame out the top of the horse because we like her zebra legs. We want to pretend we're in Africa for our Instagram.' So I said, 'We can do better than that.' We took Lily around to that back paddock and I got a great photo of the four of them. They were sat having a pretend picnic on the grass with zebra legs in the background. It looked ace. I mean, totally weird because you could only see the legs, but they were happy as anything and stuck a tenner in the jar on the way out. Lily, of course, loved the attention. You know what she's like."

"Wow," said Mariella, thinking deeply. She was unusually quiet as she wheeled the tandem out of the workshop and paused to prop it up on the side stand.

"Girls, we've got £1,000 to make today. What's going to be more likely to get us there – fish finger sandwiches or a zebra?"

Chapter 13

Lily the Zebra

"First rule of business: give the customers what they want," Mariella announced.

Rosie squinted slightly, racking her brain as to where her mum could possibly have dredged up this rule after years of completely dismissing business as a game played by 'pinstripe money-hoarders'. She wondered what the second, third and fourth rules were, but she was excited to see her mad mum back in all her powerful glory and didn't want to ask questions that might break her stride.

Mariella continued: "If they want a zebra, that's what they get. Cass, go get Lily. Rosie, can you find that non-toxic spray paint we bought for marking the animals when we went to the county show?"

The girls laughed and went off to search for their items.

Lily – technically grey, although a non-horsey person would call her white – was a former racehorse who had been reasonably successful on the track. Only about a third of racehorses are female as, like most mammals, the male of the species is a touch taller and has a longer stride. The fact that Lily had taken on the boys and won was one of the reasons Mariella had adopted her when she had become too old to race. What made her so popular with the customers of Cranmore Donkey Sanctuary was not her racing pedigree but her eagerness for attention. If she saw a camera, her instinct was to trot over and photobomb it. Mariella assumed it was a throwback to the days when she received an enormous fuss when she won a race and the photographers would snap her picture.

"Right, Cass, you take the lead here. Let's get these stripes right."

Cass began to lay out strips of material onto Lily's back as stencils and sprayed thick lines of black in between them. She referred back to a picture of a zebra on her phone, ensuring she got a smooth transition from the vertical stripes around her body to the horizontal stripes on her socks. Lily's ears flopped forward as they did when she was happy, and she gave approving grunts as Cass worked.

Meanwhile, Mariella and Rosie headed off to the bakery in Cranmore for supplies. They tried to calculate how much bread, ham and cheese to buy, but it was so hard to predict how many people might come. Eventually they just bought as much as they could fit on the tandem, with baguettes sticking up out of the paniers like flag poles.

Approaching the gates of Cranmore Donkey Sanctuary, they burst into laughter at the sight of Cass struggling with a huge sheet of plywood. On it she had painted a picture of a grinning zebra, holding a smartphone in its hoof. Above it were the words:

#zebra-selfie

and a large black arrow pointing left to show the entrance to the car park. Mariella and Rosie parked their tandem, and together they got the sign nailed to a lamppost. They all walked back around the corner into the park, pushing the heavily laden tandem between them.

"Cass, before we open, can you put '£5 entry' on the sign? Also, can you write 'Coffee, sandwiches, cake'. I know for years we've not even charged an entry fee and meekly asked for a £2 donation. It seems nuts to charge £5. Then I think about taking £1,000 in a day and we just have to be ambitious. If it doesn't work, tomorrow we'll lower it. Now, you going to show us your handywork?"

Mariella and Rosie's jaws fell to the floor when they saw Lily the Zebra. She looked stunning, with thick black bands snaking around her body, and a diamond of thin black stripes that Cass had carefully hand-painted down her long face. Lily padded over eagerly to show off her new look, and the three of them got into position around her for the first selfie of the summer.

"This is it, girls. The start of day one. Say CHEEEEESE!"

At 10 AM the gates opened and the three of them nervously waited to see if anyone would come in and pay £5.

Chapter 14

New Beginnings

The first vehicle came in shortly after they opened: a van full of builders looking to buy some sandwiches. Mariella had not yet finished preparing the food, so the guys sat in their van while she made them to order. For years she had avoided talking about money, too uncomfortable to even ask people to make donations despite knowing how essential they were. As she bagged up the lunch, she and Rosie calculated it should be £4 for a coffee and a baguette, so £16 in total.

"Shall we call it a tenner, Rosie? Sixteen pounds seems so much for lunch," Mariella suggested.

"Mum! Weren't you all like 'the first rule of business' just one hour ago? I bet they normally go to the petrol station and pay that for a soggy old sandwich. It's all good."

Mariella smiled and took the paper bag out towards the car park, but their van was empty. She returned to the yard and found them hanging out with Cass, giggling like kids as they took turns to take selfies with Lily.

"Don't forget to tag Cranmore Donkey Sanctuary and hashtag zebra-selfie, yeah?" said Cass. The builders nodded obediently, tapping away at their phones.

"My kids will love this," said one of them. "They always wonder what I do all day. Now they'll know I just pop off on safari!"

The lads gratefully received the bag of sandwiches and tray of coffees. "We use fresh baked baguettes, thick ham from local farms, organic milk and proper fresh ground coffee from the machine," boasted Rosie.

"Wow, they look fantastic. Here's £20 for lunch and £20 for the selfies. Good luck! We'll be back tomorrow."

It was a huge confidence boost to have taken £40 before 11 AM. Mariella disappeared back into the kitchen to make more baguettes and bake a chocolate cake. Unfortunately, baking was not one of her strengths. She had caused havoc at Rosie's fifth birthday party when she had accidentally used salt instead of sugar in the donkey-shaped cake. The only edible part was the icing, and all the kids had fought over the ears.

By lunchtime, several more families arrived and made no fuss about paying the £5 entry fee. Rosie and Cass put all their love into the guided tours, letting the children lead the donkeys for a walk around the pasture. Later on in the afternoon, a family posed by Lily and asked Rosie the inevitable question.

"So, is it an actual zebra? It's awfully tame."

"There are three sub-species of zebra: Grevy's, plains and mountain," Rosie said, trying to dodge the question.

"Right, and which one is this?" the mum asked.

Cass came bowling over and interjected.

"It's a horse! It's a horse painted with non-toxic paint to look like a zebra. If we put a zebra here, then it would be dangerous because they're wild animals. By using this horse, we can allow kids to get up close to it and explain the differences. Rosie, can you, er, explain the differences?"

"Absolutely!" Rosie said with relief. The lie had made her feel a bit sick and now she was back in her comfort zone, sharing her knowledge about animals.

"Lily's legs are long – she used to be a racehorse – but a zebra's legs would only be about as long as their body is deep. You see her pink muzzle. On a zebra that would be black. Another giveaway is her tail. Lily's tail is a bundle of hair, but a zebra tail is solid like a dog's, with a bit of hair coming out of the end."

The family were delighted with the facts, and Cass made a mental note of them for her next tour.

That evening, Cass stayed for dinner of leftover cheese and ham rolls. Mariella counted the day's takings.

"Two hundred and twenty-three pounds after we take off the cost of the food. Girls, that is amazing! I mean, it's not £1,000, but it's double what we used to make in a day. So, adding a zebra doubled our appeal. What next? We could borrow another grey horse from one of the local stables and do another zebra? I bet Maureen would let us borrow Martha?"

"Mum," Rosie replied, "I don't think it works like that. People are only excited about the first zebra, then they're like, 'What next?'. If we had twenty zebras – even if we had twenty *real* zebras – it would be just like when we had twenty donkeys. Once you've seen one, you've seen them all. By the way, that's me doing an impression of the visitors; don't give me a huge lecture about how different all their personalities are."

"Ha!" laughed Mariella. "You know me too well. Fair enough. And there's only so many ways you can paint a horse. What else can we do?"

Chapter 15

Dam Realistic

Rosie awoke to find a note on the kitchen worktop that said:

Out in the pond.

In the pond? she thought, curiously.

Outside, she found her mum wearing dark green waders, waist deep in the large pond that sat in one of the fields. About the length of a bus and roughly circular, it had taken Mariella weeks to dig it out by hand a few years ago. It was now a haven for dragonflies, frogs and visiting herons. Mariella stood in the middle of it, grappling with a huge branch.

"Morning, Rosie!" she shouted. "I bet you're probably wondering what I'm doing in the pond."

"Yes! What are you doing?"

Mariella barely paused in her work, wrestling the branch onto a stack of other sticks that seemed to float in the middle.

"Guess!" she shouted back to her daughter.

"Hmm. If you're building a raft, it might be easier to do it at the edge and *then* launch it," Rosie supposed.

"Nope!"

"You're pulling sticks out of the lake?" Rosie guessed again.

"No, the opposite," her mum shouted back, wading towards the edge to gather more sticks.

"I'm building a lodge!" she finally revealed.

"Cool! Are we getting a beaver?" asked Rosie excitedly.

"Well, we're getting a beaver *lodge*. I haven't thought any further than that!" her mum said, wading back into the lake with another armful of sticks she had gathered.

Rosie went back inside and looked online for a beaver for sale, but she only found a lot of coats.

She and Cass, who had turned up for a coffee before her shift started, were horrified to find that a real beaver's fur sells for only about ten pounds. They quickly felt bad for having considered rehoming a beaver in rural England. They did, however, find some adorable webcam footage of a beaver inside its lodge.

Cass jumped up excitedly.

"Hey, Kittywhiskers," she said to Rosie, "what if we have a shed that overlooks the beaver lodge. Inside the shed is a television that plays this video of the beaver on a loop. We say to the kids, "See that lodge there? There's a camera inside it and you can watch what the beaver is up to on this television." Meanwhile you can tell them all about the way they build their dams and all that malarkey."

"Yes!" replied Rosie, pausing as she took it in. "That's perfect. It's a bit sneaky though, isn't it? Saying we've got a beaver, when really we've only got a video of a beaver we found on YouTube."

"Yes, it's a bit wrong, isn't it," Cass pondered, sitting back down. "Thing is, they really *are* seeing a real beaver on that screen. It's just that the beaver is a lot further away than they realise. And it was recorded ages ago, not live. It's not *that* bad, is it?"

"Well, it's not super honest. But I guess it's only for a few weeks, and we have to do whatever it takes to save this place."

"Exactly. And it means people get to see a beaver without us having to take one away from its mum."

At this point, Cass did an impression of a lonely beaver, moping around the lounge with an oven glove tail and calling out 'Mommy!' in an American accent. Rosie laughed and they went to tell Mariella, who thought the idea was genius and, after all, wasn't *that* much worse than the zebra lie.

Cass, experienced in creating video installations, worked with Mariella all weekend to clear out a shed near the pond and transform it into a lookout point. The shed's sign read 'Beaver Shack', painted in white on wood that Mariella had blackened with a blowtorch. One internal wall displayed a huge map of the world's remaining beaver habitats, together with a poster entitled 'The Real Cost of Fur'. The opposite wall held the television from Rosie's bedroom, showing a three-hour loop of a beaver asleep and then pottering about in its lodge. Rosie had requested the friendly owner of a beaver sanctuary in Canada to send her all the raw footage he had. When Rosie had asked if it was okay to use his video, he had been happy to help a fellow animal rescue centre. She told him if he ever needed a video of a donkey asleep, he knew who to ask. He politely assured her he would keep her in mind.

Mariella had cut out a window from the side of the shed that faced the pond, and from this panoramic viewing point the beaver lodge looked fantastically convincing. A pile of interwoven sticks and branches the size of a small car, it sat like a mini iceberg, half above the surface of the water and half below.

Sunday night marked one week since Peter had given them the dreadful news about losing the farm, leaving just five weeks to raise the money to save it.

"How were takings today, Rosie?" Mariella asked as she loaded the dishwasher.

"Well, compared to a normal Sunday they were fantastic – £443, and we normally do about £100. Compared to our goal of £1,000 per day, well, not quite there yet. But still, we're hanging in there. Cass has been so brilliant with the visitors and doing selfies. Have you seen Lily's Instagram account? She has 250 followers."

Mariella peered through the window between the kitchen and dining table. "Wait – so we have a horse masquerading as a zebra, and she has more followers in one week than the park itself has gained in years? Wow!"

They laughed and headed off for bed. Rosie carried a stack of printouts about beavers, ready to educate the world tomorrow in their brand-new beaver exhibit.

Chapter 16

Busy as a Beaver

On Monday at 10 AM, Cass opened the ticket office to find two families already waiting in line. She smiled, as she had never seen this happen before in her years of helping out at the sanctuary. She explained that they would be the very first people to see their new beaver, fresh off the plane from Canada, and walked them over to the Beaver Shack.

"It says on the sign 'Alaska'," said the dad of one of the families. "So which is it, Alaska or Canada?"

"Great question. Well, our beaver actually lived on the border and swam between the two countries," Cass boldly explained.

"But Alaska's not a country," the man said.

"Okay. Thanks for your feedback." Cass smiled, remembering her time at the call centre. If it gets tricky, just smile and go back to the script. "Here's Rosie, who will tell you all about him."

Rosie turned the tour around, confidently explaining how beavers are second only to humans in the way they can adapt their environment, gnawing down huge trees and damming entire rivers. She passed around a log that the dad could barely reach his fingers around and explained how a beaver could gnaw through it in under ten minutes. Rosie pointed out that beavers were mostly nocturnal – truthfully – and the family happily watched the 'live feed' of the animal nestled in its lodge. They cooed when it briefly woke up and snuffled around, and the dad told his kids to keep their voices down as they walked past the lodge towards the donkey paddock.

"Mum, the beaver exhibit is a hit!" Rosie exclaimed over lunch. "Look at this review we got this morning on Tripadvisor. It reads: *Five stars.*

The beaver is so cute, and the young guide taught us loads of good facts. More than just donkeys."

Mariella took the phone and reread it several times, beaming with pride and hugging her daughter. "That is fantastic."

Then the sparkle disappeared from her eyes, and Rosie immediately sensed the change in her mood.

"What's up, Mum? I thought you'd be stoked."

"I am, Rosie. It's just when I see all these happy visitors and we're taking £400 per day, I keep thinking, 'This is how it should have been all this time.' I realise now we could have made this place successful years ago, and I didn't because I just did the same old thing, day in, day out. That girl who came in a few weeks ago was right – my zoo sucks. Or at least, it *sucked*."

"But Mum, we can still do this, right? Even if we don't have the whole £40,000 by the end of summer and only have half of it, surely it'll be enough to prove to the bank we can do this and just need a little bit more time?"

"Yes, I bet you're right, Rosie. Look at that review you got this morning; a few more like that and we'll become a hit local attraction and catch up to our goal. I'm sure if we're close, the bank will give us some more time. After all, Peter must be on our side – he's our bank manager. You're doing such a brilliant job, Rosie; I couldn't be more proud of you. I kind of wish your dad were here to see how well we're doing."

Chapter 17

Rob

Visitor numbers remained strong. By Monday afternoon there were small queues forming to get a selfie with Lily the Zebra and to watch the 'live' feed of the beaver. Not one guest had questioned whether the beaver was actually there in the lodge. Rosie had her routine down to a fine art, and any doubts about whether they were doing the right thing were long forgotten.

More reviews trickled in, raising their Tripadvisor rating from 2.8 stars to a more respectable 3.5. In a moment of quiet triumph, Cranmore Donkey Sanctuary was now ranked above McZoo in "Things to do with kids in Westingbury".

For years, the sanctuary had been a quiet backwater where people stopped to eat their picnic on the way to somewhere better. With more to see at the park, visitors were now spending hours there and buying food and drinks. Mariella was run off her feet preparing sandwiches and baking cakes, and even squeezing lemons from their greenhouse to make authentic lemonade.

Their shopping list had outgrown the carrying capacity of their tandem and the local bakery was happy to deliver their growing order to them.

They were all so busy that Cass decided to call some of her friends to see if anyone would voluntarily help out. Her good friend Rob was always ready for an adventure, and he arrived to help out on the ticket booth the following day.

Rob was eighteen and lived in Westingbury, where he went to the same college as Cass. He was good looking with messy blond hair and broad shoulders. He was fiercely independent, and being a wheelchair user that meant he had developed a powerful instinct for problem solving.

Rob had met Cass at a music festival on the Isle of Wight, where they were both waiting near the entrance to see if anyone had a spare ticket they could buy. They started chatting and realised they were both from the same town, and both needed to catch the last ferry home. Unfortunately nobody had a ticket to sell them, and with just a few hours to go before they had to leave, their thoughts turned to sneaking in to catch a band or two.

Rob noticed that the security guards were only giving an occasional glance to the river of people leaving the festival, focusing mostly on the people coming in.

"Cass, if we tried to sneak in through the exit we'd get busted straight away. We'd be facing everyone else coming out and when the security dude glances over, we'd stand out like a sore thumb."

Cass shrugged as if to say 'well, duh'. She wondered where he was going with this.

"But if we face the outside world," he continued, "at a glance we'll look like one of the many people leaving the festival. So, let's go to the exit and go *backwards* into the festival against the flow."

She laughed and the two of them casually reversed their way into the festival, slowly making their way backwards as a swarm of people overtook them on all sides. Once inside they had a blast watching bands, then racing to catch the last ferry back to the mainland with seconds to go.

When Cass called Rob to see if he wanted to help out at Cranmore Donkey Sanctuary for free, he felt like it was karma. Spending a summer manning a ticket booth was his come-uppance for having fiendishly avoided buying a ticket that fateful day. Mostly, though, he just wanted an excuse to hang out with Cass.

Taking more than £500 on a Monday was a phenomenal start to the week, but Mariella knew she had to redouble her efforts to get the daily profit up to £1,000. She and Rosie spent the evening poring over an animal encyclopaedia to get ideas for what to add next. After a flicking through all 844 pages, Mariella shut the heavy book and sighed.

"How can we do it though, Rosie? We obviously can't buy an actual animal because they cost a fortune and we'd have to build all the enclosures, pay vet bills, etc. We can't hire wild animals because... well, this isn't Hollywood. All I can find online is taxidermied animals and I just hate the idea of having a dead animal. Even if we get away with pretending it's alive – somehow – we don't know how it died and it might have been cruelly hunted and shot in the first place. We can't start out as an animal sanctuary and end up with trophies from a Victorian hunting trip."

Rosie agreed, and they sat in silence in the lounge for several minutes. Finally, she had an idea.

"Remember when I went to Hannah's house last year. Did I tell you about her dog?"

Mariella shook her head.

"So we went up to her bedroom to play and I sat on her bed, and I heard a muffled yelp. I realised I'd sat on something and stood up to see it was an animal. A little puppy curled up on Hannah's bed. I was like, 'Oh! I'm so sorry, little one,' and I began stroking it. It was a husky pup about the size of that cushion, with its head on its paws and eyes shut. Meanwhile I noticed Hannah starts sniggering, which was odd because I thought she'd be more concerned about her dog."

Mariella was now sat up on the couch, intrigued. "So, it was a toy, right?"

"Yes! But so much better than a usual fluffy toy. It was seriously so realistic. The fur on it was coarse and not as soft as on a cuddly toy. Its ears had that leathery feeling you get on a real dog, and when you stroked its head its ears kind of rotated slightly like real dogs' do. It had loads of different yelps and barks when you stroked its tummy, and even raised its head slightly when you rubbed its muzzle. So naturally we got talking about her amazing dog and it turns out she'd wanted a puppy forever but the whole family is allergic to dog hair, so her grandad surprised her one day by making it. I kid you not – he made it in his shed. Apparently every year she sends Grandad a picture of what toy she wants for Christmas, and if she doesn't specify a link for where to buy it, he'll just construct it from scratch. Princess castles, radio-controlled boats, anything."

"We have to find him, Rosie!" exclaimed Mariella. "He sounds amazing."

Chapter 18

Torsten

The next day, Mariella and Rosie gobbled their breakfast, got on their tandem and rode to Hannah's house.

Hannah proudly demonstrated her husky pup to Mariella, who was awestruck at its realism. Mariella explained that she would love to meet the puppy's creator to discuss potential work for him. Hannah's mum called her dad – Torsten – to let him know they were on their way. As they left, Hannah shouted, "Ask to see his trains!"

Twenty minutes later, Mariella and Rosie pulled up outside Torsten's house and knocked on the door. It was only 9 AM on Sunday morning, but clearly Torsten was an early riser, as he answered the door in a pair of smart trousers, a waistcoat and bow tie.

"Hi, you must be Rosie and Mariella," said Torsten, with only the slightest German accent remaining after living in the UK for his entire adult life. "But I'm afraid you might have got the wrong person. I am retired now. Still, please come in and have some coffee in the garden. I am intrigued."

They sat in the shade of his beautifully neat garden, where every plant was meticulously pruned and the edges of the flower beds were sharp and precise.

"Before we explain, can you tell us more about your background? We saw the amazing husky pup you made for Hannah. Did you do work in movies or something?"

He laughed and explained that he had been a civil engineer all his life, designing bridges and motorway overpasses. "I would have certainly loved to have a job in the movies, but I don't have a creative bone in my body. Only numbers and maths," he said humbly.

"Would it be possible to see your trains, please?" Rosie asked politely. Torsten shifted uncomfortably. He hesitated and turned to his wife, who nodded encouragingly.

"Oh, okay. As you're a friend of Hannah, you can come. I don't really show people this because once they see it they will probably think I am a crazy person or something."

He led Mariella and Rosie down an immaculate garden path to a double garage and stood aside as the door swung open. Inside was a vast landscape at waist height stretching from wall to wall. It was the biggest and most impressive train set either of them had ever seen, with train lines carved into rolling grassy hills, and tunnels snaking through mountains and pine forests. Mariella and Rosie were so hypnotised by the scale of the construction that they didn't speak.

A walkway cut through the middle of this alternative world. Only as they walked through it did they begin to appreciate the intricacy of the model's details. Streetlights glowed and trainline signals flashed intermittently. Stations housed little figurines the height of a fingernail. Bushes and trees lined the streets. Rosie could imagine Torsten using a cocktail stick to paint each tiny leaf.

"And this is you *not* being creative?" joked Mariella.

"I can only copy things," Torsten replied. "This is my home village where I was brought up, in Bavaria."

Torsten pointed to a map of the area, which he had meticulously recreated down to the position of phone boxes. He had even used aerial photographs of the region taken in the 1970s, to get the precise details such as his former neighbours' swimming pool and the playground in his school. It was an incredible work of art and feat of engineering.

After marvelling at the model for some time, Mariella told Torsten that Cranmore Donkey Sanctuary was broke. She explained how the bank manager had dropped the bombshell that they must raise £40,000 or lose the farm, and that the one glimmer of hope was that they were now making a daily profit for the first time in years. The 'zebra' was a hit and they desperately wanted a boa constrictor because it would be impressive yet barely move.

Torsten thought for a while and said, "I am sorry, but I think you need a professional person who knows what they are doing. I made that puppy for Hannah but do not have enough experience to create a good enough item for your project. I am sorry I cannot help you."

Mariella and Rosie felt deflated, but they thanked him for showing them his incredible train masterpiece. Torsten began to show them out of the house and wished them well in their project.

As they left, he noticed their tandem and was intrigued by it. He crouched to look at the metalwork and carefully inspected the joints between the tubes of the frame.

"Did you weld this yourself, Mariella?" he asked.

"Yes," she replied. "I found it in the tip and had to rebuild it because it was all twisted and bent."

"You did a wonderful job. One of the first things I built as a child was a bicycle because I was sick of the walk to school. I made it from steel and it was so heavy that I would get to school sweating. But to glide down the hills on the way home was the greatest feeling."

Mariella was beginning to do up her helmet and swing her leg onto the tandem when she stopped. She kicked the stand back down, returning to Torsten.

"Torsten, think about the Bavaria of your childhood and how simple life was back then. That

104

feeling you get; it's not just about riding a bike down a hill. Everyone's done that. It's that feeling of the freedom you had – you had a problem and you solved it. I'm the same as you – I just want to build and create. We're not asking you to come and do a stuffy job with rules and measurements and clocking in and out. Yes, you're right, the sensible solution would be to pay thousands of pounds to ask a big movie prop company to build us an animatronic snake. But we're not sensible. We're a donkey sanctuary hanging by a thread, doing whatever it takes to survive. We don't have thousands of pounds, we're not in Hollywood. We're here, in your front garden, and we're asking you because we think you're obviously the most talented and creative engineer we've ever met. We believe you can do it, even if you don't."

Torsten smiled nervously, then turned around and walked back into his house.

Mariella sighed. It wasn't the first time she had frightened someone off with one of her rants. She fastened her helmet and began to wheel her bike down the driveway, feeling thoroughly disappointed.

"Come on, Rosie," she said. "Let's go hatch a plan back home."

"Wait, wait," shouted Torsten, moments before they pulled away. He hurried towards them, showing the clipboard and pen that he had gone inside to fetch. "I need to know the species you need," he said with a warm smile.

Chapter 19

We're Gonna Need a Bigger Fence

Torsten worked day and night on the snake and kept texting extraordinarily specific questions to Mariella, such as, 'Should it look like it has recently been fed?'. When he contacted her on Wednesday morning to ask how long the power supply cable should be for the tank, Mariella realised she had not even thought about where it would go. She spent the morning clearing out a workshop to convert into a reptile house, piling all the tools into another shed and sweeping it out. She knocked up a table out of scrap wood and made a large sign over the door saying 'BOA CONSTRICTOR'.

At lunchtime she was bewildered to see a woman aged about 70 standing in the main yard with a tray of sandwiches. "Can I help you?" Mariella asked politely.

The woman turned and said, "No, can I help *you?* I've got ham, cheese, or ham and cheese. For drinks I can do coffee or tea. What would you like, love? It's £5 for coffee and a baguette."

"Okay. Well, I suppose I should introduce myself. I'm Mariella. This is my park."

"Ooooh, lovely! I'm Cass's nan. She told me all about you, and I said I wanted to help out. I don't know a thing about animals, but I can make sandwiches. It's nice to meet you, Mariella!"

They both laughed, and Mariella thanked her profusely for helping out. "So, what shall I call you?" she asked.

"You can call me Nan."

There were now five members of staff at the sanctuary: Mariella, Rosie, Rob, Cass and Nan. At any given time there were ten to twenty visitors walking around the park, petting the donkeys or taking a selfie with Lily. Meanwhile, Rosie repeatedly introduced people to the world's second largest rodent – who didn't seem to want to leave its lodge today, again.

That afternoon, Rosie bounded up to her mum excitedly.

"Mum, I've got an idea which is epic, and you've got to trust me. Okay? I can't tell you all about it, you just have to trust me."

Her mum was intrigued, and Rosie had certainly built up plenty of trust over the years.

Rosie led her mum down through the donkey paddock towards the bottom of the farm, where they reached a stone wall. They called the area beyond that wall the 'Lower Field', but it was more wild woodland than grassy paddock. The triangular copse was contained on one side by the border to McZoo, on another side by hedgerow and on the top side, where they stood, by the long stone wall. It was dotted with ancient beech and oak trees, and up near the wall it transitioned to tall meadow grass with purple thistles and burdock.

"Mum, I need you to build a fence *on top* of this wall, so it ends up two metres tall. I know it's a long wall, and it'll take a lot of fence posts, but it's going to be worth it, I promise. I've got something soooo good. Do we have enough fencing for that behind the main shed?"

"Yes, I think we probably have enough, but you know it'll take me all of today, and probably tomorrow too, to get that up. Are you sure we need it? I mean, what are you intending to put in there, a T-rex?"

Rosie grinned and shook her head, refusing to give up any details of her plan. Her mum sighed, smiling lovingly at her daughter.

"I trust you. Okay, I'll crack on. If you need me, you know where I am."

That evening, Mariella came indoors at 9 PM and collapsed onto the sofa, having worked for six hours straight putting up fencing. Rosie brought over her dinner, which was a ham and cheese roll. This time she had microwaved it because she felt it made it more of a 'dinner' if it was hot. The cheese had melted but the bread had gone chewy. Still, her mum was grateful not to have to cook and ate two in a row.

"I've finished that tall fence," she said in between bites. "Are you going to tell me now what's going in there? I've been racking my brains

110

all afternoon. Something that jumps high? Kangaroo?"

"Nope. And you'll have to wait till tomorrow morning to find out. Goodnight Mum. I know I don't need to tell you to sleep well – you look like you'll be lucky to make it off the couch and crawl to your bedroom!"

Chapter 20

Gorilla Man

"Aaaagh!" screamed Mariella as she pulled open her curtains the next morning. There in the yard, just a stone's throw from the house, was a gorilla!

Rosie ran into the house, laughing wildly. "It's okay, Mum! It's not a real gorilla. It's just a guy in a gorilla costume. You were wondering what we needed a tall fence for? Well, here you go. That's our new exhibit. A full-size silverback. I wanted to get him into his new enclosure before you woke up, but it worked better this way anyway. I haven't heard you scream in… hmmm… ever!"

"Oh, my goodness. Who is he? Where did you find a guy with a gorilla suit? Do I even want to know?" her mum asked, heart still pounding. The weirdness soon passed over her and she wandered into the kitchen.

"Does he want a coffee? Tell him the kettle's on."

Rosie led Gorilla Man down to the huge field that would become his habitat for the whole summer. Before the park opened at ten, Mariella went down to introduce herself, only to find Gorilla Man running off, unwilling to let her get near.

"Mum, he won't talk to you. He's a method actor and takes his work very seriously. He even plans to sleep here at the park, in his enclosure. He said it was now a piece of performance art, and that was the last thing he would say to me. He's committed to stay till September. I said you'd build him a little cabin to sleep in and we'd bring him food. He said he only wanted bananas. I mean, this guy is serious about being a gorilla!"

"Where do you find these people?" laughed Mariella. "Here's me thinking it was weird yesterday to find Nan had come into our kitchen and baked a cake. By the way, Rosie, these

'Electric Fence' signs are a brilliant touch, and I see why it had to be so tall."

Gorilla Man had disappeared into the patch of trees that would be his home for the summer. It was far enough away from the fence that sometimes he was difficult to spot, hidden amongst bushes. He walked on all fours and explored his surroundings, sniffing convincingly at trees and bashing the ground occasionally with sticks. The park had not even opened yet.

The first few visitors arrived at 10 AM and were blown away to find a gorilla had been added to the animal line up. As usual, Rosie gave a fantastic tour, managing to inject it with the same level of energy even after doing it dozens of times each day. She explained that humans share about 98% of their DNA with gorillas, but she felt a little awkward knowing that in fact they shared 100% with this one in particular. Like the zebra and the beaver, the lie became second nature and quickly did not feel like a lie at all.

The next day Torsten arrived, looking nervous. It was only four days since they had met him for the first time, and by some miracle he had already finished the boa constrictor.

He explained to Mariella that it was heavy, so she opened up the gates and he drove right into the park and to the reptile house she had prepared. As she walked over to his car, he said that he was sorry he was not able to do a better job and it was not quite right. He was happy to take it back and make changes if she thought it was not good enough.

When he opened the boot of his BMW, Mariella was taken aback by the creation. The back seats were down to squeeze in a fish tank as long as a person. Inside was a boa constrictor so lifelike she was nervous to reach in and touch it. Its eyes were glossy and black, its skin perfectly textured with tiny scales and painted a greeny-brown. Its thick body – as fat as a toilet roll at its widest, with a head the size of an avocado – looped forward and back in the tank on a bed of leaves, sand, rocks and branches. The foliage convincingly obscured the snake, and inside the lid was a yellow light.

"Torsten, this is just so perfect. I can't believe you constructed that in four days. What's it made of?" beamed Mariella.

"Really? Oh, great. Phew. Well, the body is chicken wire and papier-mâché, which is what I use to make all my landscapes on my trains. So I have some experience working with it. The head is a single block of clay, which I sculpted by hand, copying some pictures from books. The skin was the tricky part; I painted it in liquid latex and dragged in some texture lines as it dried. Then I painted it with an airbrush kit. Oh, and for the tongue I used a small servo – a little motor that is meant for periodically making a train gate go up and down. You'll see when you plug it in."

Cass had joined them by this point and was also dazzled by the realism. "You're my hero!" she declared to Torsten, who blushed.

The three of them lifted the tank out of the car and carefully carried it into the shed. When they plugged it in, the yellow light turned on, bathing the snake in a warm glow. Every 30 seconds its tongue flickered and retracted, giving it a fantastic realism.

Mariella thanked Torsten again and was amazed at how generous he had been with his time. He even refused to take any payment, saying that the only cost had been the fish tank, which he'd bought online for £40.

With that, he left. The sanctuary was beginning to feel more like a small zoo, with its zebra, gorilla, boa and beaver.

Chapter 21

A New Record

"Went to see donkeys, found a gorilla. Awesome!" Rosie read out the latest review on Tripadvisor as she and Mariella ate dinner together.

"I've got something even better than that," announced Mariella. "Today we took £724! Can you believe it, Rosie? I can't."

"Mum, that's insane!" replied Rosie. "Does that mean we won't lose this place after all? We'll be able to pay back the bank, right?"

Mariella explained that they had a long road ahead of them. So far they had made nearly £5,000 towards their goal of £40,000. They were nearly two weeks into their six-week notice period. If they could keep up this momentum all summer, and the money kept going up every day, there was a glimmer of hope.

"My main worry at the moment is people, as always. So far, we keep giving them new things for their Instagram. We've been adding something every day or two. But we can't keep that up all summer, can we? In the end, everyone around here is going to have visited, and are they really going to come back again and again for that zebra selfie? I think they'll save a fiver and repost the original photo."

Rosie agreed, soberly, before perking up again when she remembered they'd made over £700 in ONE day.

"Anyway, speaking of the next new thing, Torsten called me today," continued Mariella. "I told him how over 200 people had already seen his boa constrictor and not one of them questioned whether it was real. He was chuffed to bits and said that making his train set felt a bit boring after the snake. Wondered if we wanted another animal! I said yes, and that I'd talk to you."

They agreed that what worked so well about the boa constrictor was the fact it was an animal you are used to seeing motionless. The more an animal moves, the more obvious it would be that it's fake, so they brainstormed slow-moving animals. They came up with a tortoise, chameleon and other reptiles, but decided they would be a bit similar to the boa. Snails – even a Giant African Snail – probably would not draw the crowds. There was a moment of pensive silence.

"SLOTH!" blurted Rosie.

"Yes Rosie! You've got it. A sloth will be brilliant!" her mum agreed excitedly, ideas flooding her mind. "We could stick it up a tree somewhere, put a fence around it and boom! People would spend ages spotting it!" She stood up to do an impression of a visitor trying to tell someone where to look, peering up at the ceiling and saying, "Look at that branch on the left. Now count two branches up, and you see a little V. Follow that to the left. Behind the leaf. There. That's its bum."

Rosie doubled over laughing as Mariella searched for her phone to call Torsten.

Meanwhile in Lower Field, Gorilla Man was bedding down for the night in a makeshift cabin that Mariella had cobbled together from a few pallets. It was tucked away out of sight in the trees and had a pillow and duvet. She would have appreciated a 'thank you', but Gorilla Man stayed true to character and scarpered to the other side of his enclosure while she did her work.

As darkness fell, Mariella peered out of the cottage window and shook her head at the eeriness of having a fake gorilla sleeping at the bottom of the garden. She double locked the door that night, for the first time in years.

Chapter 22

An Unwelcome Visitor

The last few days of that week were hectic at the park. The car park was consistently half full and there was a constant row of people along the gorilla fence, pointing down into the trees and zooming in to take photos. At lunchtime, Rosie delighted the guests by wheeling down a barrow full of fruit to toss over into the enclosure. She wished he would catch it, but Gorilla Man never broke character and just sauntered about in the shadows, occasionally picking up his meal and taking it back out of sight to his cabin. Very rarely did he come up towards the fence, presumably because up close it would be obvious that his legs were too long for a gorilla, and his shoulders not tall enough.

Mariella was beginning to recognise the same families coming for repeat visits, and the money was coming in so thick and fast that even Nan was now accepting contactless payments for sandwiches. The oven was on from 7 AM till 4 PM to keep up with demand for freshly baked cakes, and the bakery delivery each morning was now coming in huge sacks. For the last five days they had made over £700 per day. Their original daily goal had been to make £1,000 for 40 days, and although £700 was close, Mariella knew that every day they missed their target would mean later on they would need to be making double that to stay on track. It seemed unthinkable, even after all her recent success. Still, she focused each day on feeding the animals and solving the constant problems that came with a park full of guests.

The feeling of joy at the park was short lived when a familiar dusty Jaguar rolled up at lunchtime and Elvin McEadly demanded to speak to Mariella. "Tell him I'm at golf," she joked to Rob over the walkie-talkie, before reluctantly going to meet him in the car park.

"What the hell do you think you're doing?" Elvin spat as she approached. He prodded his finger in the air, hissing, "I've been running my zoo happily for twenty years and we've never had a problem with you and your little donkey show round the corner. But now you're not happy with your lot anymore, are you? No, now you want what I've got. Well let me tell you, it ain't going to happen!"

"How dare you come into my park and tell me what I can and can't do," Mariella retorted. "Do I come round to your place and tell you to feed your animals properly? Or that their cages are cruel and too small? No, I mind my own business, and so should you."

"Oh, but you DO stick your nose in, don't you?" He walked towards Mariella with a venomous look in his eye, his words cutting the air like a knife. "I know you destroyed my fence and broke into my zoo. I know you stole one of my animals."

"*Your* animals? That's rich! My poor Esther – who you said you'd look after, 'one conservationist to another'? The donkey you shoved on a concrete floor in a dark barn and got ready to feed to your malnourished lion? Ugh. You are just a profit-hungry circus master pretending to be a conservationist because otherwise everyone would see your zoo for what it is. A prison."

"Right." Elvin nodded mockingly. "And yet it's fine for you to keep a gorilla in a field? Who do you think you are, Mariella? You need to remember your station. Anyway, what do I care? You won't have this place for much longer."

"What are you talking about?" she snapped, wondering how he could possibly know anything about her financial affairs.

He paused, grinning as he got back into his car. "We'll see what happens, won't we? Hey, don't worry; I might hire you to clean out my lion. I think he'll be making a right old mess when I feed him sixteen donkeys. He can't wait!"

With that, he closed his window and accelerated, gravel spraying back towards Mariella. Elvin pulled onto the main road without looking carefully and a truck had to brake, beeping at him as he sped off up the road.

Chapter 23

After Elvin's Visit

Mariella was shaken up by her encounter with Elvin McEadly and vented to Rosie while Nan put the kettle on.

Rosie asked how he seemed to know about the bank threatening to sell the farm from under their feet. Mariella called Peter, who assured her that their financial affairs were held in the strictest confidence and that he had no knowledge of Mr McEadly whatsoever. She asked if the deadline could be extended if they were able to raise part of the money. He hurriedly said he had another call and hung up.

It was a sombre morning, and after two cups of tea, each accompanied by a slice of Nan's delicious carrot cake, Mariella put on a brave face and pulled on her red wellies. She knew that despite what Elvin had said, they were still making more money every day. While the gates were open there was a chance that they could save the farm before the end of the summer holidays.

Later that Sunday morning, the park was fairly busy and Rosie was giving a tour, starting with the beaver pond. She explained that sadly the beaver was in its lodge today, but the family could go into the lookout and watch him on the live video feed. When she got to the Beaver Shack there was a young woman there, about Cass's age. The girl was transfixed by the live feed, and it was the first time Rosie had seen a customer bring their own camping chair.

"Oh, hi. I wasn't expecting to find someone already here. Are you okay?" Rosie asked.

The girl jolted up in her chair, surprised by the intrusion of the group, and flipped over a notepad that was on her lap so that Rosie could not see what she had written.

"Ah, you're an artist? Cool," said Rosie.

127

The girl looked confused, then looked down at her notepad and smiled. "Oh. Yes. Love drawing. Don't mind me."

Rosie thought nothing much of it, and she continued the tour on to the gorilla enclosure. The group could see the gorilla walking around on all fours deep in the woods, occasionally slumping heavily onto the grass and toying with a stick or flower.

"How come you ended up with a gorilla at a donkey sanctuary?" asked the mum of the family she was guiding around the park.

"ZooBay," Rosie said, regretting it immediately. She had heard Cass give this explanation once before, and she could not think of anything better. "It's a website that's kind of secret and you won't find it on Google. Zoos trade animals, and this gorgeous gorilla from a zoo in Bavaria was for sale, so we snapped him up."

"That's interesting," said the woman. "May I ask how much it was?"

Rosie froze up, having no clue how much a gorilla might cost and finding herself backed into an inescapable corner. She wondered what Cass would do in this situation and remembered her trick of switching into call-centre mode when things got tough. Rosie relaxed and moved to an irrelevant autopilot script, delivered with a vacant smile. She found that after a few confusing detours, the 'caller' would soon give up and move on.

"Yes. It's a mountain gorilla from Rwanda, and there are only 1,000 left in the wild due to awful human conflict and deforestation."

"Right, but I just wondered how much one pays for a gorilla. It seems so strange that you can go on ZooBay and buy a gorilla," the lady persisted.

Rosie cringed a little as she delivered her next call-centre reply. "Did you know that gorillas are afraid of water? They hate the rain, and they only cross rivers and streams if they can find a log to balance on. Now, shall we go and see Lily the Zebra?"

The mum gave up. "Yay!" said her kids, and off they went to take selfies.

Chapter 24

Sloth Arrives

The next day was Monday, marking a full two weeks since their fateful meeting with the bank manager. Mariella's mood perked up when she got a text from Torsten saying the sloth was ready. She spent the morning working down by an old oak tree near the beaver pond, erecting a fence around it while Rosie made a sign with a map of South America showing the sloth's natural range.

"Torsten, considering sloth means 'slow', you were extremely quick with this one!" said Mariella, rolling her eyes at her own bad joke. As with the boa, the accuracy was stunning. Its two-toed front claws were made around stiff wire so they could be bent to grip any branch. Its fur was shaggy and browny-grey, and Torsten explained that he had bought some wigs online and then rubbed them with dirt and wax to get the matted look. Torsten had used a black nose from one of Hannah's old teddy bears and the sloth's face was adorable. It looked perfect, and Mariella and Rosie knew that tucked away in the tall branches of the oak, nobody would ever suspect it wasn't real.

They took the sloth into the house because they needed the park to be empty before they could go up a ladder and hang it in the tree. It sat on the sofa and made Nan jump when she came in to take a cake out of the oven.

Over the first two weeks, the amount of money they made each day kept rising. Thankfully, almost all their takings were profit, since nobody was getting paid. Mariella had promised that if the business survived then they would all have a job for life. Nobody quite knew if that was a promise or a threat, as their jobs had become a quite bizarre charade of leading people around a series of fake animals. Still, they were all enjoying their summer because there was always some funny story about customers asking difficult questions and the team nearly getting busted.

Later, Cass approached Rosie in the yard. "Have you seen that girl in the beaver shack?" she asked. "It's her second day there! Is she writing a book or something?"

"Wow, is she still there?" exclaimed Rosie. "I assumed she was drawing a picture. She did bring her own chair, so I should have known she planned to stay a while."

The two of them plotted to find out what the girl was doing there by sneaking over to the Beaver Shack and peeking in through the window. They planned to creep quietly to the side of the building that faced the pond, knowing that the mysterious girl's attention would be on the screen and not the window. They thought if they sat on the grass under the window, they could rise up and sneak a look at the girl to find out what she was jotting on her notepad.

"She'll bust us if we stand up like that," pondered Rosie. "It'll be so obvious."

"Leave it with me, Tiger Chops!" said Cass, whizzing off towards Lily's selfie area where she was used to spending most of her day. Cass returned with her phone on the end of a telescopic pole about as long as her arm. "Selfie stick!" she cried.

132

The two girls waited till the ten or so park visitors appeared to be eating their lunch. They could see from a distance that the secretive artist was still inside the Beaver Shack, so they made their way towards the pond side. They crept through the long grass and finally reached the side of the shed overlooking the pond. They sat under the window, convinced their heartbeats would alert the girl who was just the other side of the thin wooden wall.

Cass switched her phone to silent and fired up the camera, hitting the red circle to begin recording. They would not be able to see what it captured till they watched the video later. Cass carefully raised it up to the height of the window like a periscope. Rosie had to hold her hand over her mouth to stop herself from giggling, convinced that at any moment the girl would walk around the hut and discover the two of them sat in the grass looking ridiculous with their selfie stick. After what felt like minutes, Cass slowly lowered the camera back into her hands and stopped recording. The two of them crawled out of their hiding place towards the main yard. They could not wait to see what the video would reveal and so rushed to Rosie's house to watch it.

133

Cass's video showed the shack girl staring intently at the live feed of the beaver. On her lap was her notepad and – curiously – a stopwatch. Cass's video only lasted 23 seconds, and in that time the mysterious character had jotted down one or two words, which they were unable to read. Rosie and Cass were no closer to knowing why she was spending so much time in the shack, but they were left with an uncomfortable feeling about it. The fact that she was timing something was particularly odd.

Over dinner that night, Rosie recounted the adventure to her mum.

"You think *that's* weird?" asked Mariella. "Did you see the boy at the gorilla enclosure counting fruit?"

"Was he about 15, wearing a baseball cap?" replied Rosie. "Yes, I did see him there several times today. I just assumed he liked the gorilla. What makes you think he was counting fruit?"

"Because I went down there at lunchtime to throw in the fruit and he literally stood by me doing a tally on a clipboard as fast as I could throw bananas over the fence. It was bizarre. I guess he's doing a school project about the feeding of gorillas," said Mariella.

"Ah yes!" said Rosie with a sense of relief. "I bet that's it, Mum. I bet they're doing biology coursework and have to look at animal behaviour. That's probably what the girl in the Beaver Shack was doing, too."

It was only 9 PM, but the days were so long and exhausting that this was now the normal time for them to retire to bed. Mariella kissed her daughter on the forehead and went off to get a well-earned sleep.

Chapter 25

Queen's Official Business

Rob called Mariella on the radio with urgency in his voice. "Mariella, you need to come to the front office immediately. We have a situation. Over."

It was Thursday morning and the park had several families dotted about. Mariella ran towards the Portakabin, where Rob simply pointed the aerial of his radio towards the blue Jaguar in the car park.

"Oh no!" cried Mariella. She sped out to stop Elvin from coming any further into the sanctuary.

"Mariella, do not try to stop me. I am on important business on behalf of the Queen and Courts of Great Britain. Come on, Mr Dawson!" Elvin shouted, tapping aggressively on the window of the car parked alongside his own.

From the neighbouring vehicle a man sheepishly emerged, wearing a pastel blue cardigan, brown corduroy trousers, sandals and socks. He carried a clipboard and was clearly uncomfortable at being ordered around by McEadly. Mr Dawson opened the boot of his car and brought out a tripod and what looked like a large video camera, almost homemade in its simplicity. It had a plain grey plastic shell and a carry handle on top, with a curly cable that led to a battery pack. On the side it read 'Thermo-Matic' in orange lettering.

"This is Mr Dawson from the Inspectorate of British Zoos," announced Elvin, articulating every letter with a ridiculous sense of self-importance. "We have reason to believe you, Mariella, are in breach of the code of conduct of the zoos of Great Britain."

Mr Dawson nervously nodded his head at Mariella, before being ushered by Elvin towards the entrance.

"I believe the sloth in question is this way, Mr Dawson. Chop chop," he said.

By this time, Rosie was at her mum's side. "Mum!" she whispered urgently as if to wake her out of her shock. "Did you see what he got out of his car? That's a thermal imaging camera!"

"Okay. And what's the point of that?" Mariella asked, out of earshot of the two men crunching their way across the gravel car park.

"I don't know, but they said they were going to the sloth!" said Rosie.

"Oh drat!" Mariella replied. "They want to prove it's fake by showing it has no body heat!"

Mariella sprang into action, squeezing the button on her radio and talking under her breath so that the two intruders would not hear.

"Urgent. Rob, Nan, everyone – hold up the two men who just walked into the park. I need at least five minutes before they reach the sloth."

With that, Mariella sprinted from the car park towards the yard, leaping over a gate to avoid going past the ticket office. Meanwhile, Rob wheeled himself down the ramp from the office and into the path of Mr Dawson and Elvin.

"Excuse me. You need to buy a ticket," he stated confidently.

"Buy a ticket? What are you talking about, son? We are working at the highest government level to maintain the greatest zoos of any country in the world. Do you have any idea how important this man and I are?" said Elvin McEadly furiously.

Cass and Nan arrived at the scene, joining Rob and Rosie. "You need to buy a ticket, so let's go this way to the ticket booth and buy a ticket," Cass said calmly with a wide smile.

Rosie giggled nervously.

"Are you listening to me, girl? I'm Elvin McEadly!"

"I don't care if you're Belvin McTweedly or the Queen of England. You need to buy a ticket!" said Nan, who was blocking their way with a tray of cakes.

Elvin shook with rage and turned towards the door of the office. Rob – who in his spare time took part in wheelchair races and could move faster than any of them – darted towards the ramp and got there first. He then slowed to a snail's pace and inched his way up it to the door. Elvin tutted noisily and peeked around as if threatening to overtake.

Once inside, Rob cruised over to a box of wristbands and took one out, slowly rolling back towards Mr Dawson.

"Come on sunshine, we haven't got all day. Sell me a blasted ticket!" shouted Elvin.

Meanwhile, Mariella had grabbed a ladder and was racing through the park towards the sloth. Several guests were stood around the base of its oak tree, pointing up and trying to spot it. "Excuse me please!" said Mariella as she hopped over the wall and leaned the ladder against the trunk.

"What are you doing?" asked a young girl in a red dress.

"The sloth is not very well, unfortunately. I need to give her some medicine," Mariella said as the ladder bashed against the trunk and she began to climb up.

Back at the office, Cass was deep in call-centre mode, explaining in a patronising tone where the fire exits were in case of an emergency. Elvin practically screamed at her to sell him a ticket, to which she replied, "No problem, sir," before continuing with a painfully detailed description of where to find the toilets.

Elvin threw his hands up in dismay and walked towards the door to head into the park. "That's it. I'm going in whether I have a ticket or not!"

Now it was Nan's turn to block his path. "No you're not," she stated simply. "What would the Queen say if she knew her loyal subjects were flaunting her laws?"

"That's exactly why we're here," he spat. "You're the ones flaunting the law! You've got a fake sloth, and I'm going to prove it!"

"Not. Before. You've. Bought. A. Ticket," she told him calmly. "Now would you like a slice of carrot cake while you're waiting?"

Elvin's eyes nearly popped out of his head with rage and he slapped a £10 note on the counter. Mr Dawson checked he was not being watched and pointed politely at the cake, handing £2 to Nan from a bag of coins in his pocket.

At this point, Mariella was high in the tall tree and able to see the entire park. She unhooked the sloth from its branch and hung it around her shoulders like a baby. "There you go, little one. Let's get you some medicine," she said softly, hurrying down the ladder and vaulting the wall before sprinting towards the house.

"It must be very sick," the little girl said to her mother.

Mariella flew through the bungalow door and into the kitchen. She popped open the microwave and stuffed the sloth inside, cranking the dial to five minutes and hitting the button marked 'Potato'. The light came on and the machine burst into life, rotating the sloth's face so its nose squished against the glass. Blue sparks crackled from the animal's fur, and Mariella knew that, since it contained metal wire, the appliance might blow up at any second.

Back in the office, Rob was still stalling Elvin. "I've just got to go get some change from the main office," he told him.

"What?! This IS the main office. She's got change. Get it from her, you buffoon!" Elvin pointed his bony finger at Nan, who had a Tupperware container brimming with coins.

"You're not having *my* change," Nan insisted. "Cakes is a whole different department. We'll be in a right muddle if we start moving money around willy-nilly, won't we, Cass?"

"You're absolutely right, Nan. The mountain gorilla shares 98% of its DNA with us humans and is the most closely related mammal to us after chimpanzees and bonobos," said Cass with a smile.

There was silence for a second before Elvin screamed.

"I've paid. I'm going. Get out of my way, you fools! Keep the blasted change!"

Pushing past Nan and exploding out of the office door, he strode forcefully down towards the sloth enclosure. "Elvin McEadly coming through on important government business. We have a warrant," he shouted at anyone who would listen.

Elvin arrived at the bottom of the sloth's oak tree. "Here it is," he called to Mr Dawson, who had finished his cake and finally caught up. "Set up that equipment of yours and I'll prove once and for all that it's a fake sloth in this fake zoo run by a fake businessperson."

"It's not well," revealed the little girl in the red dress to Elvin.

"Oh, is that right? You know why?" he said, crouching to look her in the eyes in a rare moment of apparent empathy.

She shook her head innocently.

"Because it's made of wood. Now clear off! We've got men's business to attend to."

143

The girl's mum gasped in horror and put her arm around her daughter, leading her away. Meanwhile Mr Dawson had set up his thermal imaging camera and pointed it up into the tree. He looked into the screen, noting some measurements on his clipboard. Elvin paced forwards and back, biting his nails in anticipation.

"It's absolutely conclusive, Mr McEadly," he said after a pause. "That sloth is very much... alive. Look, you can see there it has a strong temperature reading. In fact, that little girl was right – if anything, it's got a slight temperature."

"It's not possible!" Elvin fumed. "Check it again! Your blasted machine is broken!"

Mr Dawson packed his equipment away, clearly irritated by the accusation that his readings were incorrect.

"I checked it twice. My machine is fine. Now if you'll excuse me, Mr McEadly, I have actual work to do and I don't appreciate being dragged out in what is clearly a spat between two neighbours. Good day." He turned to Mariella and his face softened. "Thank you for the cake, Ms Harpel."

Elvin screamed and stormed off back to his car. He got in, slammed the door, then revved its engine so hard that plumes of black smoke belched out of the exhaust pipe.

The workers at Cranmore Donkey Sanctuary cheered from the office as Elvin disappeared around the corner. Rob, Mariella, Rosie, Cass and Nan had never felt closer as a team. The intercom was abuzz for the rest of the afternoon as they relived key moments from the escapade. Mariella joked that she had some official Queen's business to attend to, but Rosie could tell her mum was a little shaken by this latest scrape.

It was clear that Elvin was on the warpath.

Chapter 26

The Truth About Zebras

Rosie and her mum relaxed on the sofa that evening with hot chocolate. There was no television to watch anymore because it was being used in the office to keep an eye on the yard. So they just chatted.

"Do you think we're doing the right thing?" Mariella asked. "I looked out today and there was a family happily taking selfies with Lily. Family are happy, Lily seems happy. I mean, she can't talk but she could easily walk back into her stable if she got sick of it, like Bella does every day. So everyone's happy. Still, it just doesn't feel quite right."

They were both so exhausted after working in the hot sun, and their encounter with Elvin, that the conversation happened in slow motion with long pauses between each thought. Rosie lay on the yellow sofa. Its corners had been ravaged by their cat, who used it as a scratching post despite Mariella having made her a brilliant one in the shape of the Eiffel Tower. After some consideration and having completed the first, white layer of her Rubik's Cube, Rosie replied, "Are you worried that they realised it wasn't really a zebra?"

Her mum was on the rust-coloured sofa, which for some reason was not popular with the cat. It had sunk in the middle like a hammock, but it was supremely comfortable after a day of hard work.

"No", Mariella replied after some thought. "I think I'm worried that they *did* fall for it. They thought they were buying one thing, but they got something different."

Rosie thought for a minute or two, manoeuvring the cube quickly in her nimble fingers. "But whether they know it's a horse or think it's a zebra, they got what they paid for," she replied.

Her mum stirred her hot chocolate and sipped it, before trying to explain her unease. "Rosie, imagine you saw the Mona Lisa in Paris. You'd feel ripped off if you found out later you'd seen a replica. I'm not even sure why that is."

Rosie had now completed two layers of her cube and was working on the yellows. She methodically ran through algorithms – rotating one side and then another – which she had memorised years ago from the booklet that came with it.

"Perhaps it's the rarity," Mariella continued. "Zebra – in the UK at least – are rare, and rare things are valuable. Horses aren't rare."

"True," Rosie agreed, "but horses painted as zebras are super rare! So I think it's okay."

"You may be right, Rosie, but we need to be honest and let people decide for themselves. They might think, 'Oooh, a horse painted as a zebra. I want a photograph!', or 'Tosh! I'm not paying £5 to see a painted horse.'"

Rosie placed her completed Rubik's Cube on the coffee table. She half rolled over to look at her mum over the arm of the couch.

"Mum, why is it that when you do an impression of a customer, you do it as if they're an upper-class gent from Victorian Britain?"

Mariella burst into laughter, knowing it was true and she had no idea why. Rosie continued:

"In your mind you must imagine that our guests waddle in with a walking cane and a top hat, fresh from a fox hunt with the Duke of Westingbury. 'How do you do? I came here to look at the zebra. Tally-ho.'"

Mariella laughed hard for the first time that day.

"What is wrong with me, Rosie? How long have I been doing that for?"

"Forever! 'How do you do? Whence can I cometh and see one's famous tepid sloth?'"

They both were in stitches, taking turns to do impressions of a Victorian man being amazed by the fake animals at the park.

When the laughter simmered down, Mariella returned to the original conversation.

"Thing is, I can't bring myself to confess it's all made up. We're making money – finally – and the hope of saving this place is all that's keeping me going right now. What if the truth ruins everything?"

Rosie agreed that they must keep up the pretence for just a few more weeks.

As it happened, that would not be an option.

Chapter 27

Knockoff Zoo!

It was Saturday, and two days had passed since the zoo inspector had visited. Mariella and Rosie had risen early with big expectations for the day ahead. They were chatting and making breakfast when there was an unexpected knock at the door. There stood Hannah, Torsten's granddaughter who was also Rosie's friend from school. She was on her bike, wearing a bright yellow safety vest and with a huge neon orange bag of newspapers slung over her shoulder.

"Hi, Hannah," said Rosie, giggling with confusion at her friend popping round at half past seven in the morning. "To what do I owe this early morning pleasure?"

"I just went to pick up the papers for my round and I saw this. So I came here first. I'm so sorry, Rosie," Hannah said with a worried look, thrusting a rolled-up newspaper into Rosie's hands, before swiftly cycling off.

Mariella unrolled it on the kitchen table to reveal it was the *Hampshire Gazette*. The headline, in huge white letters on a red background, read: "KNOCKOFF ZOO!" Mariella and Rosie both felt sick to their stomachs as they recognised the photo of Lily on the front page.

They sat still for what seemed like an eternity before Mariella took a deep breath, plucking up the courage to begin reading the article out loud to her daughter.

A special investigation by the Hampshire Gazette has evidence that Cranmore Donkey Sanctuary near Westingbury is deceiving its customers with fake animals. Owner Mariella Harpel has owned the facility for ten years and appears to have reinvented her donkey sanctuary for the summer season as a zoo, presumably to compete with the nearby McZoo. Among the list of animals added to the park are a 'zebra' that is quite clearly a horse [pictured]; a gorilla, which we believe is a human in a costume; a mechanical snake; and a beaver that is simply not there. In our two-page exclusive exposé we uncover the sham in full.

The article went on to show photos of the gorilla alongside a photo of a real mountain gorilla. It was fairly easy to see that Gorilla Man had longer legs and a smaller torso. It said that 'evidence that had been anonymously provided to the newspaper' showed that the gorilla had consumed an average of just four apples and ten bananas per day. A real gorilla, by comparison, could eat ten times that amount.

The newspaper went on to show four identical screenshots of the beaver, looking up at the camera with its teeth on show. The timestamp on each image showed that the pictures were taken on different days. This proved it was the same piece of footage being looped over and over.

"Oh no," said Mariella, her voice trembling. "This is so bad, Rosie. I mean, we have to shut the park right now because by the sounds of it we're breaking the law. I'll go and lock the gate."

Rosie gave her mum a hug and reminded her that people loved the park and all the new animals. In her opinion they had not done anything *that* bad.

As Mariella hung the 'Closed' sign on the gate, she heard the huff and puff of Cass's old car limping up the lane. She opened the gate and let her in.

"Why are we closing?" asked Cass.

"Oh Cass," Mariella sighed, "just wait till you see the local paper." She linked arms with Cass as they headed to the bungalow.

"Knockoff Zoo?" Cass said. "Yeah, I saw that on Lily's Instagram account. People keep posting pictures of her on the front of the paper. But do we have to close? No different to the Natural History Museum, is it? They have stuffed animals. So what?"

Mariella explained that by being open for the last few weeks without making it clear that the animals were fake, they had potentially broken the law. As the newspaper had screamed, it was a breach of public trust and a violation of the Trading Standards Act, which is set up to make sure businesses describe honestly what customers are buying.

"You know Elvin McEadly's at the bottom of all this, don't you?" said Mariella. "Remember that kid counting the apples and bananas? And that girl who sat in the Beaver Shack for days on end? I bet they work for Elvin. I bet he packaged up all the evidence and gleefully sent it to the paper. I can see the look on his face. He probably wrote their exposé for them."

Mariella put her head in her hands and began to sob. Rosie rubbed her back while Cass went to make tea and find a packet of biscuits.

"I've well and truly blown it, girls. I'm going to feed the animals."

Chapter 28

I've Blown It

All morning Mariella's phone rang, pinged and buzzed as people tried to contact her. The reaction on social media was a mixed bag to which Cass tried to reply as well she could, mostly using call-centre mode to say the park was shut till further notice.

Some locals on Cranmore Donkey Sanctuary's Facebook page were clearly never deceived in the first place. "If you didn't realise that was a horse you need your eyes tested!" said the top comment. Some were even more impressed now they knew the truth and wanted to come and see Gorilla Man again to bring him a hot lunch. Others clearly fallen for the charade and felt like they'd been 'treated like a mug', as one person put it. The comments came pouring in, and #knockoffzoo began to trend on Twitter.

By lunchtime, the story had moved from the *Hampshire Gazette* to the BBC News website. The reaction from those who had never visited was more favourable, with most people making fun of anyone who had been so easily conned and giving kudos to Mariella for having pulled it off. Several offers came in to buy the boa constrictor from people who had always wanted a snake but didn't want the hassle of feeding it.

By late afternoon somebody had set up a fake Instagram profile for Gorilla Man, where you could supposedly hire him to 'live in your garden for up to two weeks'. The cost? 100 bananas.

Lots of news outlets pestered Mariella for an interview, and a couple of reporters showed up at the gates, but going on television now was the last thing on her mind. She was heartbroken and wanted to be on her own. She spent as much of her time as possible peacefully sweeping the yard as she tried to make sense of it all.

She had run the sanctuary for ten years. It had mostly been a joyful time with Rosie and John. It was endless work and they never had money, but it had been the best place in the world to raise their daughter. Mariella knew that all her problems were because of her terrible business sense. For so many years she had done nothing to reinvent the park or improve it. She kicked herself as she remembered that when she saw the income dwindle to almost nothing, instead of trying to improve ticket sales she created a vegetable garden so she would not need to buy as much food. She had always thought that profit was a dirty word, and then finally, when she decided to make some money, she did it all wrong and ended up on the front page of the paper.

Mariella was sitting on a hay bale and crying when Rosie came in.

"Fish finger sandwich?" asked her daughter, offering a plate. Mariella nodded affectionately. They sat side by side and stared at the stone floor.

"Oh Rosie, what a mess I've made," Mariella sobbed. "I lost your dad over this stupid place. Now I've lost our home. It's all gone and it's all my fault. I'm too useless to run a business. I can't even cook dinner."

"Don't worry, Mum. We've still got each other. We can find a new place to live and it'll all be okay." She gave her mum a squeeze. "By the way, I texted the others and told them the park is closed and that you'd call later on."

That afternoon, Mariella turned her phone back on and deleted all 200 messages without reading them. Rob and Nan sympathised and thanked her for a wild ride. Mariella called the bakery to explain why there would be no more bread orders this summer, and the kind owner, June, said not to worry about the newspaper story. Back in 1995, she explained, her bakery got shut down because food inspectors found a rat in the kitchen. "It'll blow over," she reassured Mariella, who could only think about how many ratty baguettes she had eaten in the last few weeks.

"Mum, there's one more person to tell," said Rosie, pointing down from the house towards the bottom of the farm where Gorilla Man had spent ten nights.

"Oh gosh, forgot about him! Yes, going now."

She pulled on her red wellies and made her way down the path, over the gate and into his enclosure. Gorilla Man had no phone and no idea why the park had been so unexpectedly empty that morning. He was sat on a fallen log near to his shack.

"You can take it off now," she called as she approached. "The park's closed. For good."

He remained silent with his gorilla head on, and Mariella shrugged, sitting next to him on the makeshift bench.

She went on to explain how Elvin McEadly had orchestrated an elaborate sabotage and now she had to close the zoo and rehome her animals. That included him. Gorilla Man listened, thumbing a long piece of grass in his long black fingers as his boss began to get emotional and let her thoughts pour out.

"It was never going to work," Mariella continued, finding it surprisingly easy to open up to a man in a gorilla suit. "It was a stupid idea. How was I ever going to run a successful business that involves making customers happy, when I don't understand people? I thought I did, too. That's what kills me! For one precious moment last week I looked out and thought, wow, this is really cool. People are having a good time. They're not wincing at putting a pound in the donations jar, they're actually paying and they're coming back again and again.

But of course, it wouldn't work out because I'm not cut out for business. No matter how much I change this place, I can't change myself. I mean, a leopard can't change its spots, right? You can't even change out of your gorilla suit."

Mariella began to sob, so Gorilla Man stretched out his huge, silvery-black, hairy arm to place around her. She recoiled for a second as the looming shape approached. Then she relaxed and let the heavy limb rest on her shoulders. The fur tickled her skin and he smelt like a wild animal, but she felt safe nestled in his strong arm.

"See, I'm fine with animals!" she said between sobs, eking out the first smile of the day. "Just not people. My ex-husband. Amazing guy. Never really loved this place, and I tried to change him but couldn't. People are who they are."

Gorilla Man pulled his arm away from Mariella and stood up. He put his rubbery black fingers up to his face and slowly began to pull his gorilla head off. For ten days Mariella had only seen him as a gorilla, so now she felt like she was witnessing a huge animal decapitate itself. The head came off with a pop.

"People *can* change, Mariella. You already have. More than you know."

160

"John?! What?"

Mariella froze as she saw her estranged husband standing there in his gorilla suit. His hair was a sweaty mess and his skin was pale from being covered for so long. He stank like she imagined a real gorilla would.

"It's been you all this time?" she said, dumfounded.

He nodded, and tears rolled down both of their faces.

"Sweating away in that gorilla suit all summer long. You... you don't even like bananas!" she said, standing to walk into his open arms.

They both laughed as he pulled her in for a powerful embrace. She gripped him back, squeezing his matted fur.

Meanwhile, Rosie was watching the whole time with binoculars from the wall with the fake electric fence.

John and Mariella sat back down on the log, feeling light-headed and slightly dazed by the flood of emotion.

"Why did you do it?" Mariella asked.

"When Rosie told me she was looking for a guy in a gorilla suit, I thought, well, there's something I can do. Yes, I know I used to resent this place

161

because it was taking you away from me. But when Rosie told me all the things you were doing, it sounded so exciting. I badly wanted to be a part of it. I knew you'd be stressed out with it all and the last thing you needed was me waltzing in trying to be your business partner again. So I thought, here was my chance to be a part of it, you know, without causing any issues."

Mariella smiled. "Wow. And you have lived on a diet of apples, bananas and nuts for the last ten days?"

"Yes," he said. "I'd see that lady with a tray of baguettes and think how badly I wanted one! Tell you what though, I feel amazing! I'm gonna write a book called *The Gorilla Detox*!" he added.

"Well, you can have a well-earned bacon sandwich, because it's over. Turns out you were right all along. I suck at business," she said.

"I never said that! I just wanted to have dinner with you once in a while. You say a leopard can't change its spots, but seriously, look at this place. You built this in a matter of weeks. We had more guests here yesterday than we had all of last summer, and those kids are having the time of their lives. I am so proud of what you've done. Don't let anyone convince you that you suck at

162

business, or that you're finished. You are just getting started!"

"Aww, thanks, John. Really, thank you so much for trying, and for being part of this. Now, can you go and have a shower please?"

Chapter 29

The Tortoise

Over the weekend the phone gradually stopped ringing and things quietened down on the farm. Mariella had accepted defeat and begun boxing up her items in preparation for moving out. Rosie spent the weekend at her dad's, so for Mariella it was a lonely and emotional two days of sorting through items that reminded her of the good times she'd had at Cranmore Donkey Sanctuary. Although business had eluded her, seeing all the photos of Rosie splashing in puddles and playing with animals reminded her that she was a great mum. John's words about kids having the time of their lives at the sanctuary kept resurfacing in her head. She began to wonder if business and motherhood weren't so different. Maybe running a leisure attraction was about extending your parenting to other people's kids.

Mariella had always felt like business was a game played by *other* people, a party to which she wasn't invited. In her mind was an outdated stereotype of a greedy man, hawking a shoddy product and spending his energy shooting down any newcomers. Being muscled out by Elvin McEadly had reinforced that stereotype, and worse, she was now passing it on to Rosie. She shuddered at the thought that this whole episode could make Rosie also grow up feeling like business is a game for *them*, not us.

On Sunday morning, Mariella took down a picture from the living room wall ready to bubble-wrap and put in a box. In the photo was five-year-old Rosie in her rainbow pyjamas. She was curled up in a ball on the bedroom floor with a plastic washing basket on her back, pretending to be a tortoise. Mariella could almost still hear her giggles.

Flopping on the rusty-coloured sofa, Mariella stared at the picture in her hands. If there's one thing I can definitely do, she thought to herself, it's help kids have fun. And if kids are having fun, we have a business. And if we have a business, we can save the farm.

She put the photo back onto its nail on the wall and got out her permanent marker, looking around for blank surfaces on which to scribble.

Chapter 30

Who Wants More?

That evening, Mariella emerged from the kitchen with a tray that clinked with mugs of tea. She was followed by Nan carrying a stack of plates and a large coffee cake smeared with thick white chocolate buttercream. On the yellow sofa sat Rosie and Cass, with Rob alongside. Perched on a stool was John, affectionally stroking the cat. On the rusty couch was Torsten, in a smart waistcoat and his trademark bow tie. He was the only person to have brought a notepad, a pen and a freshly sharpened pencil.

Nan passed round the cake and tea, and the room went quiet as Mariella stood to face the group. Having only phoned them that afternoon, she was thrilled that they had all made it.

"Thank you for coming back at such incredibly short notice," she began. "I know this summer has been a rollercoaster, going from queues of people one day to being disgraced on the front page of the newspaper the next. I didn't know if you'd all have the stomach for another twist and turn."

"Wait, there's more?" joked Cass. "I'm just here for the cake!"

"Bless you, Cass. No, the cake doesn't come for free! The thing is, that evil scumbag Elvin McEadly wants me to give up. My own bank manager clearly thinks I should give up. The *Hampshire Gazette* seems to agree with them both. But what about the customers? I was looking through photos on my phone this weekend and it's all smiles everywhere. We're up to 4.8 stars on Tripadvisor! In amongst all that madness, we were doing *something* right, and I can't give up now with three weeks still on the clock. I have to try, and I've got an idea that might convince you to rejoin me."

The team sat forward in their seats, listening intently. They had expected to come for a group hug and reminisce at photos from the last few weeks, but this was starting to sound like a war cry. They were intrigued and excited to hear how their boss felt she could possibly turn things around.

Mariella yanked down a sheet of brown wrapping paper that had been Blu-tacked to the wall. Written in black permanent marker on the paintwork behind it was the word 'Financials'.

"We made about £10,000 in the two weeks we were running before we got shut down," Mariella continued. "That's incredible. Now we have three weeks left and need to make £30,000. So simply reopening isn't going to cut it – and apparently it would be illegal. We need to do something that will triple the daily profit. *Triple*." She repeated the word slowly so everyone could truly grasp the scale of the task ahead.

Mariella stepped aside and pulled the next piece of brown paper from the wall to reveal the words:

OPERATION TORTOISE

- Land

- You

- 1 week build (£10,000)

- 2 weeks profit (£40,000)

"This the mission, should you choose to accept it." Mariella grabbed a wooden spoon from a pot on the kitchen worktop and started to work through her list, pointing at each item as she spoke.

"We've got this land. We've got the greatest team in the world. We've got £10,000 to spend on building something incredible. If we spend one week building something, that will give us two weeks to make the money to save Cranmore Donkey Sanctuary before the deadline."

The team nodded energetically, shovelling down cake and licking the icing off their fingers. Mariella continued, tearing down another sheet of paper to reveal the word 'Strengths' followed by a list.

"I went through all our online reviews and pulled out all the specific things that kept coming up. Not the usual stuff that every tourist attraction has like 'easy parking', but the unique superpowers that only we have. This is the stuff that has to be a part of whatever we create."

Mariella pointed at the first item on the list with the wooden spoon.

"Number one. Rosie's animal facts. People learned a lot about animals – not just kids, their parents too. Rosie, you have an incredible gift for making learning fun. That needs to resonate throughout everything we do, from the signs to the tours."

Rosie turned red with embarrassment at the attention, and Cass hugged her with sisterly pride.

"Number two. Hiding the sloth. It was like Elf on a Shelf! People spent ages just standing there looking for it up in the branches. Combining animals with a game gave visitors a challenge, and they loved it.

"Number three: zebra selfies. This was your stroke of genius, Cass. It gave people an Instagrammable moment to make their day memorable. At the same time, it provided free advertising to the park. Just brilliant.

"Number four: Gorilla Man. You are *still* trending on Twitter, John! You staying in character for ten days is the grossest, weirdest, most marvellous thing. The public love you for it, and so do I." John blushed, and Cass passed him a banana from the fruit bowl.

"Number five: Nan's cake."

Rob put his hand up, so Mariella paused and nodded so he could interject.

"I was gonna say – at least once a day someone would phone up to ask if they could get Nan's carrot cake delivered! It's SOOO good."

171

"Exactly!" Mariella continued as Nan beamed with pride. "Okay, number six: Torsten's incredibly life-like animals. I still feel like I have to feed that boa, and I'm sorry I microwaved your sloth."

"No problem. I should have put a heater in it," he apologised humbly.

"Next: our weaknesses." Mariella stepped across to the next sheet of brown paper, which hung to the right of the window, and yanked it to the floor.

"Number one: dishonesty. People hated feeling tricked. Fair enough. Whatever we do, we're going to be honest.

"Number two: we haven't got a licence to keep any exotic animals. Honestly, I only found out we'd *had* that license when I got the letter saying it had been revoked. Sounds like something you arranged years ago, John. No problem; we aren't going to win this by simply replacing the fake boa with a real one.

"Number three: we've got an uphill battle on the public relations front. 'Just popping over to that untrustworthy sham zoo,' said nobody, ever."

The group laughed, and Mariella came over to the lounge area to clear the plates and mugs from the coffee table. Taking her lead, the team helped ferry them to the kitchen, before retaking their seats.

Mariella disappeared to her bedroom and returned holding the model of the donkey sanctuary that Rosie had made for their fateful meeting with the bank. She set it down on the coffee table for all the group to see.

Mariella had hastily repaired the broken base of the model with Sellotape and glued the cardboard buildings back together. The major modifications were new exhibits and features scattered throughout the park, made of cocktail sticks, cardboard, Lego and string.

One by one, Mariella described what each feature represented and how it could be built. The group brainstormed energetically, coming up with improvements and other ideas for new attractions, all of which Mariella loved.

It was 11 PM when they were finished, by which time the model was covered with little diagrams, plastic animals and plasticine creations. The team sat back to marvel at the masterpiece they had designed together.

"Building this in a week will be incredibly hard work," Mariella stated. "And I understand if any of you won't be joining me for this next stage. You've all given so much already, so please don't feel obliged to keep going."

Mariella paused to see if anyone would politely bow out. Nobody moved an inch, so she continued, relieved.

"The odds are against us, but if this works, I will never forget that we built this business together. If we survive, there will be jobs with proper salaries and a share of profits if you want them."

"Ooh, salaries!" cried Cass. "But will there still be free cake?"

The group chuckled.

"I guess I'll see you all bright and early tomorrow morning then," said Mariella.

Chapter 31

The Big Push

The following morning the crew assembled at 8 AM, wearily guzzling coffee and bacon sandwiches to energise themselves. Mariella had made an even earlier start, having already fed the animals and marked out the location of the new attractions with yellow spray paint. She created sub-teams and divided up the work between them.

Cass partnered with Torsten and they took over one of the larger sheds to make a workshop in which they could build model animals. She loved learning tips from the seasoned engineer, and by the end of the first day she was diligently putting back every tool on its correct peg and measuring everything twice before cutting. As one of the only employees with a car, Cass was constantly heading off to town to load up on more wood, screws, paint and other materials. She taught Torsten a few new tricks, too. He had never used a 3D printer, and Cass amazed him by bringing hers and printing little plastic cogs for new motors that would have taken days to get sent.

John and Rob set to work on some woodworking projects, creating several sets of stilts, among other things. They cut out a window in the Portakabin office so that Rob could sell tickets through a hatch and save the time it took to serve customers inside the office.

Nan set up a textiles shed in which she churned out anything that required fabric, including some huge wings reinforced with wire. On the second day she recruited two of her friends from a local patchwork sewing club. The three of them worked quickly, fuelled by cake and tea.

Mariella and Rosie did a bit of everything, including ordering endless amounts of new tools and supplies for the team and organising the rental of a large new toilet block.

As the week went on, the park began to take shape. Music blared from the speakers from sunrise to sunset, alongside the constant din of hammers and drills. The donkeys took shelter in their stables, and only Lily ventured out to investigate what was happening. She followed Rosie and Cass around like a puppy, seeming disappointed at the sudden lack of attention.

Cass painted an enormous new sign for the front gate. The words 'Cranmore Donkey Sanctuary' no longer did justice to their new creation.

On Thursday, Mariella plucked up the courage to phone a news producer at BBC Hampshire who had left her a voicemail. She agreed to be interviewed on live television on Saturday morning, so she put a reminder on the wall of the office. They had wanted to do her interview sooner, but Mariella was insistent it had to be Saturday, hoping she could encourage people to come to the park when it reopened on Sunday.

As the week drew to a close, the revamped leisure attraction began to look unrecognisable from the tired old donkey sanctuary it had once been.

With the cost of supplies and of renting the toilet block for two weeks, Mariella had burned through all of the money she had earned in the first part of the summer. Knowing that she had spent £10,000 in one week made her feel giddy with nerves; however, she knew that she had to invest every penny she could to have a fighting chance of saving her farm.

Chapter 32

Bulldozer

"Did any of you hire a bulldozer?" Mariella asked as she looked out of the office on Saturday morning. Her team all looked out of the window and shook their heads. Mariella headed out to the car park, where a huge yellow bulldozer was reversing down off a lorry onto the gravel.

"Can I help you?" she shouted. "I think you must have the wrong address. We didn't order any machinery."

As the tank-like vehicle reached its resting place, a burly man emerged from the cab of the lorry, clutching some paperwork.

"It's for Elvin McEadly," he told Mariella, without looking at her.

"Ah, that makes sense. His zoo is around the corner; just go out of here and..."

The lorry driver cut her off. "No, it's definitely this address. Look – Cranmore Donkey Sanctuary, East Lane, SO43 2NY. That's here."

Mariella took the paper and stared at it, bewildered. The burly man handed her a set of keys.

"I'm just following orders. If that's what it says on the docket, that's where I do the drop. I have a busy day, I'm afraid, so if you've got any issues you need to take it up with Mr McEadly."

With that, he returned to his vehicle and drove off, leaving the massive bulldozer parked diagonally across six car parking spaces.

Mariella stormed into the office and phoned McZoo, demanding to speak with Elvin McEadly. "I don't care if he's at golf. Put me through to his mobile NOW!" she barked. A few moments later she was connected.

"What can I do for you on this lovely Saturday morning, Mariella?" Elvin answered, smugness pouring out of his voice. "I don't usually take calls when I'm on the fairway, so this had better be good."

"Why on Earth have you ordered a bulldozer to my park?" she demanded.

"Your park? Oh, is it not mine yet? That's right – Monday it's mine. That's when your time runs out, and you're shut this weekend anyway so it won't be any bother to you there, will it? By the way, don't worry too much about cleaning up, because we're planning to flatten the place first thing on Monday morning. Now if you'll excuse me, I must tee off."

With that, he hung up. Mariella tried to call back but the line went to voicemail.

Next she called Peter's mobile, speaking as calmly as she could, whilst raging inside.

"Peter. Elvin McEadly just dumped a bulldozer on my doorstep. Then he said he's buying my farm on Monday. What's he talking about? It's been four weeks since we met with you, and we have a six-week notice period. So can you tell him to stop trespassing and leave me alone?"

"Er… Mariella," said Peter, clearly caught off-guard. "Look, as I've said before, I don't know Mr McEadly. I'm afraid that's correct about the dates, though. If you check the letter, you'll find the six weeks is up on Monday. We haven't received the £40,000 from you and the property will be inviting offers."

"What are you talking about?" cried Mariella, now unable to hold back her frustration. "If you haven't spoken to Elvin McEadly, then how does he know all the details of our contract? If you have spoken to him about it, it would be completely unprofessional. You're my bank manager; you're supposed to be on my side, and worse still…"

"I can assure you, Mariella, that I am on your side," Peter interrupted. "As I say, I have no knowledge of this individual Mr McEadly. Now, it's Saturday and I really shouldn't be talking about work. Why don't we reconvene on Monday morning? This really isn't the time or the place for a professional conversation."

"Oh, right, Monday morning. I'll try to call you while this machine smashes my house to pieces," shouted Mariella.

With that, he hung up and switched his phone to voicemail too.

Mariella put her head in her hands and tears began to roll down her cheeks. Before she had time to find the bank letter and check the dates,

Rosie put her arms around her, squeezing her tight.

"It's going to be okay, Mum. It really is. And also," she said, grimacing at having to deliver the news, "the TV crew have arrived. Remember you agreed to be interviewed for BBC Hampshire this morning?"

Mariella's hands loosened their grip on her cheeks and her head sank down till her forehead was resting on the table.

Chapter 33

The Morning Show

Mariella paced around her bedroom trying to calm herself down and process what was happening. Rosie picked out a red short-sleeved checked shirt for her mum and rummaged in the back of a drawer for some jeans.

Mariella had never been on television before and hated the idea. She had reluctantly agreed to do this interview in the hope of promoting the reopening of the park. With this morning's bombshell that she did not have two weeks left, but only two days, it now seemed pointless. Still, she felt the need to be strong and use this opportunity to clear her name. She would put on a brave face and put an end to this unfortunate chapter of her life.

Mariella lay on the bed to pull on the jeans. "Help me, Rosie. These are tight."

"Mum, I didn't know you had skinny jeans. These are cool!" Rosie said as she yanked up on the waistband.

"They're not skinny jeans," her mum gasped, squeezing the air from her lungs to get them on. "At least, they didn't used to be."

Mariella pulled on her red wellies and exhaled slowly before swinging open the front door to face the world.

"Mariella, you look fantastic! Go get 'em!" called Cass from across the yard.

The BBC van had a satellite dish on the roof and was packed with complicated dials, knobs and screens. There were four members of staff: the camera person; a sound engineer armed with what looked like a badger on a stick; a producer who sat in the van; and a reporter who Rosie recognised from the news. The reporter was younger than Mariella, with pretty eyes, dark skin and black hair, which she wore up. She introduced herself to Mariella and Rosie.

"Hi, I'm Alyssa. This is my crew: Ella on camera, Jack on sound – when he's not at the wheel – and Jen is our producer. We're live in five minutes. During the interview I'm going to ask you some questions about the story: why you made up the animals, what you plan to do next. Then I have a couple of more specific questions that people have sent in, like, 'Did Gorilla Man really only eat bananas for two weeks?' Is that okay?"

Mariella was feeling sick with nerves, but she said it was fine, so Jack threaded a microphone into her shirt and did some sound testing. In her mind she just could not wait for this to be finished so she could hide in her house with Rosie and cry. Her dream was over, and all this work was for nothing. On Monday the pinstripe money-hoarders would come and take away her donkey sanctuary. She had not even had time to rehome the animals.

Ella counted them in: "We're live in five… four…" then mouthed the words "three, two, one".

"Good morning, I'm Alyssa Kewell reporting from the now infamous Cranmore Donkey Sanctuary, which has become better known as 'Knockoff Zoo'. I'm here with Mariella, the owner at the centre of this controversy. So tell me, Mariella – why is it that after ten years of running the donkey sanctuary you decided to suddenly fill it with fake animals?"

"I got a visit from my bank manager four weeks ago who said that, because we were behind on our payments, they were going to sell the farm. It was out of desperation really that we painted our horse Lily with zebra stripes, but the visitors loved it, as did Lily. It just snowballed from there really."

"So tell me about that moment when your bank manager said they were going to sell your park. That must have been really difficult to hear," said Alyssa.

Mariella began to relax a little. Alyssa's smooth voice and empathetic question made her feel more comfortable in front of the camera. She tried to imagine she was talking to Rosie.

"It was heartbreaking, yes. They never once phoned to say we needed to get back on track, or that it was getting serious. They just turned up out of the blue and said after ten years they were, well, breaking up with me I suppose."

"You must have been furious," said Alyssa.

"Yes, I remember swatting him with his papers as he tried to scramble out of the office. Then his foot got stuck in the floor because he had spikes on his shoes. It would have been funny if it wasn't such awful circumstances," recalled Mariella, almost smiling.

"So after the horse slash zebra, what was next?" asked Alyssa, but Mariella did not respond. Her mind was elsewhere. She looked across at the office.

"The shoes!" she exclaimed, breaking the silence. "The spiky shoes he was wearing were golf shoes!" Mariella's eyes were wide with excitement; she had made a critical connection.

"Peter is in cahoots with Elvin, and I can prove it!" she declared, turning her back on Alyssa and walking towards the workshop.

"Wait, Mariella, you're live on BBC Hampshire. Who are Elvin and Peter?" Alyssa called, following Mariella to the workshop.

Mariella swung round to face the camera. "Elvin owns the zoo next door. You know, the one with a lion cooped up in a cage so small you'd feel bad about taking your collie to the vet in it. He wants to buy my farm so he can extend his horrible zoo."

Alyssa giggled slightly, glancing at the camera with raised eyebrows and a smile. The crew kept filming Mariella as she wheeled out her tandem. Rosie joined her, grinning from ear to ear and clipping shut her bike helmet. Her mum continued, looking up periodically at the camera.

"Meanwhile, Peter is my bank manager. He claims it's totally normal to suddenly sell my property, with no warning at all. Is it heck! I think he's playing golf with Elvin right now. Rubbing their grubby little hands together at having used the small print to boot an honest working person onto the street. Elvin gets his new land, Peter gets some backhander. Everyone's happy, right? Well, I'm not happy," she stated, looking her interviewer in the eyes.

Alyssa turned to the camera and attempted to wrap it up. "Wow, this is quite a development. We've got to leave this story now as we're out of time, but perhaps we can come back and catch up later on? Back to Chris and Kelly."

Back in the studio, the two TV hosts looked dumfounded as their live story about a backwater donkey sanctuary had become unexpectedly exciting. They sat on a peach-coloured sofa, not quite sure what to do next. Chris tried to get the train back on the tracks with a link into the next scene, but it was quickly derailed again:

"Okay, we're heading over to the kitchen now to learn how to make the perfect cottage pie with our resident chef, Dani. Oh wait, hang on – the texts are flooding in that you all want to hear more from Knockoff Zoo. Alyssa, are you still there?"

Back at Cranmore Donkey Sanctuary, Alyssa composed herself in front of the camera and continued:

"I'm still here, Chris, but unfortunately we discovered that the tandem has a puncture and Mariella is frantically looking for a puncture repair kit. We might be a few minutes before… wait, what is that?"

Cass came jogging into the shot, leading Lily the Zebra – complete with full tack and bridle. Alyssa almost dropped her microphone when she saw the huge stripy racehorse join the madness. Ella the camera operator took several steps backwards to capture the growing scene.

"Mariella, you can take Lily," called Cass. "It's only two miles to the golf course; you can make it in minutes!"

Mariella dropped the box she was rifling through for the repair kit and thanked Cass, leaping onto Lily.

Rosie ran up alongside and looked up at her mum, saying urgently, "Mum, I checked the contract. It's six weeks from *receipt*. Definitely."

Her mum looked down at her daughter and blew her a kiss.

"Let's go, girl!" Mariella cried, patting Lily's neck.

Alyssa looked at the camera, almost speechless. "Are we still live? Yes, okay, so if you've just joined us, I'm here at the infamous Cranmore Donkey Sanctuary. Owner Mariella has just jumped onto a zebra and is riding it to Westingbury Golf Course, where she believes she will bust her bank manager Peter playing golf with her nemesis, local businessman Elvin McEadly. Have I got that right? This story keeps getting more wild!"

Chapter 34

Zebra on the Golf Course

The show cut to the studio. "Alyssa," said Kelly, "I'm going to read you a Tweet that just came in, and it pretty much sums up the mood here at BBC Hampshire. It says *@alyssa_k If you don't follow that zebra to the zoo I'm going to throw this television out of the window. Get in the van!*"

Alyssa laughed and jumped into the van, giving a live commentary as the whole television crew followed Mariella out of the gate. Rosie, Cass, John, Rob, Torsten and Nan raced to the bungalow and turned on the television.

Lily galloped along the grass verge by the side of the road in the direction of Westingbury Golf Course, loving being centre of attention again and expertly ridden by Mariella. At one point the camera crew lost her as she veered off, leaping a five-bar gate into a farmer's field and taking a short cut before rejoining the road a little further on.

The BBC Morning Show was going viral on the internet as people rushed to see the live images of a zebra racing around the British countryside. The van captured it all by driving alongside at over thirty miles per hour.

Within a few minutes of the mesmerising spectacle, Mariella and Lily reached the entrance of the golf course. They galloped across the car park towards a wooden sign that read *No unaccompanied women or children*. Lily leapt into the air over the sign and smashed it to pieces with her hooves, landing gracefully on the grassy fairway.

The van screeched to a halt at the edge of the car park and the door slid open. Ella the camera operator continued filming as Lily approached a groundskeeper patrolling the immaculate green grass of the golf course.

193

The former racehorse reared up in excitement. Mariella hung on and shouted down at the terrified groundskeeper, "Where is Elvin McEadly?"

"He's on hole eight, that way," the man stammered. "Madam, you can't take a horse on the golf course!"

Mariella looked back at him. "She's not a horse," she shouted, "she's a zebra. YAH!" And with that she sped off towards Hole Eight.

The producer Jen urgently told Jack to ignore the signs and just drive the van onto the grass. It was totally against protocol and she knew later she would pay the price, but this was becoming the most exciting story of her career. "Follow that zebra!" she yelled, and the van shot past the outraged groundskeeper, who shook his rake in anger.

Alyssa bounced around in her seat of the van, keeping the viewers up to speed on the story. "For anyone who has just joined us – this is the strangest story of the year. That's Mariella, who owns a donkey sanctuary. She's riding a horse, painted like a zebra. Why are we on a golf course? Because she suspects her bank manager is here right now, playing golf with her arch-enemy."

The news team caught up with Mariella at the top of a hill, where she had found Elvin McEadly and – as she had suspected – Peter. Mariella circled the two of them menacingly, looking down from her tall perch on Lily's back.

"Ah, I see. So this is you, having never met Elvin McEadly, is it?"

The two men rotated on the spot to face her, red-faced like naughty schoolboys.

"Peter, you're meant to be my bank manager," Mariella seethed, "to help me manage my banking. But what did you do? Waited for me to get behind on payments. No call to let me know it was getting serious. Nothing. Then you waited two whole weeks before you even gave me a letter saying I had six weeks' notice. Watched me squirm as we baked cakes and dressed in gorilla costumes. Had a good old laugh over a game of golf as you watched us fail. You are as bad as him."

Peter started to say something but could not get the words out before she continued.

"Well, guess what?" Mariella carried on. "Even us ladies can read small print. I have six weeks from the *receipt* of that letter: when you gave it to me, not when you printed it. I've got two more weeks to raise your filthy money."

Elvin McEadly was now fuming. "Two weeks. Two days," he shouted. "What does it matter? You haven't got the money now, and your park's shut, so you aren't going to have it in two weeks either. Just get off your high horse and let the professionals get on with the demolition."

BBC Hampshire had now been live streaming for 24 minutes, and the county was transfixed. The hashtag #knockoffzoo was trending on Twitter and people outside of Hampshire were now discovering it, logging onto BBC Online to watch the stream. There were currently over 20,000 people watching the spectacle unfold.

"That's where you're wrong. My park opens tomorrow, better than ever!" Mariella replied defiantly.

"Well, you won't be having any animals – save a few tatty donkeys – because you have lost your license to keep exotics. I saw to that," jeered Elvin McEadly with a smug smile.

"Great, because what I've built doesn't need exotic animals." Mariella paced backwards and forwards on Lily, whose head was high as she bathed in the attention.

Mariella turned her focus to Ella's camera, any unease about being on television now a distant memory. She looked into the lens with her piercing eyes. "This summer I learned that people want a great day out and they want to learn about animals. Does that *have* to involve stuffing them in cages? No. Okay, I shouldn't have faked it, but there was no cruelty at my zoo and there never will be.

"Knockoff Zoo opens tomorrow and your kids *are* the animals. Yep, you heard me right. We've got giant tortoise shells that you can get inside to experience life as a reptile. Gorilla Man is opening up his all-new treetop enclosure to your kids to play on. Experience life as a bird on our eagle zipline! Plus, of course, we're still the home of fifteen beautiful donkeys, one racehorse, and so much more."

She reached down and patted Lily, who raised her head affectionately. Mariella continued her epic speech.

"I've spent every penny we made this summer on it. We are all in, and we think you're going to love it. I've got two weeks to make enough money to get shot of these clowns for good. So for the love of animals, please come visit us," she said.

Alyssa stood next to Mariella on the golf course and looked into the camera to wrap up what had been the most incredible story of her career.

"Wow. Well, I have to say, Mariella, I don't think any of us were expecting that! You heard it, folks. 'Knockoff Zoo' is reopening tomorrow, near the village of Cranmore, and you have two weeks to check it out. Maybe more if all goes well. We will of course be following this story closely. Best of luck to you, Mariella and friends. Back to you in the studio, Chris and Kelly."

Rosie, Cass, John, Rob, Torsten and Nan had watched the whole broadcast in silence, ignoring the stream of pings and vibrations that their phones were making. As Alyssa signed off, they leapt off the sofa and hugged each other. Rosie and John could not have been more proud of Mariella, whose Knockoff Zoo was now the top trending item on Twitter.

"All right, everyone," said John. "We'd better crack on. Something tells me we're going to have a pretty busy opening day tomorrow, and there's a lot of stuff to finish."

Chapter 35

Grand Opening

Over the front gate hung a massive sign displaying the new name for the park: KNOCKOFF ZOO. It looked exactly as it did in the *Hampshire Gazette*, in white block lettering on a red background. Mariella had gone from hating that headline to seeing the funny side, and finally embracing it. She knew that by calling it Knockoff Zoo, visitors would be expecting something a bit different.

The whole team huddled in the office, all too anxious and excited to sit down. The minutes ticked down to the 10 AM opening time.

"This is it, guys," said Mariella. "We spent every penny that we earned in the first part of the summer, so we're back to zero. We've got two weeks to make £40,000. Entry price is £10 per person and a family pass for a whole year is £100. So Rob, if a family of four pays £40, ask them if they want to upgrade and come again and again. They can even upgrade at the end of their visit once they know how cool it is. Obviously, if we don't make our goal and have to close down, we'll refund the annual passholders in full."

John couldn't believe that this was the same Mariella who had so recently felt awkward about nudging the donation jar forward at the end of a tour.

"Got it, boss," said Rob, whizzing down to the car park, where he began taking contactless payments from families eagerly waiting in their vehicles. So many cars kept pouring in that Cass had to open up a spare field to make room for them all.

At 10 AM, Mariella proudly opened the gate into the park and the queue of visitors cheered, streaming in with excitement.

The Knockoff Zoo experience began with the familiar yard full of donkeys. Younger kids enjoyed petting them and sometimes leading them on a walk around the paddock. After her television appearance, everyone wanted a selfie with Lily. She had lost her stripes but maintained every bit of her magnificence. Beyond the original sixteen animals, the similarities with Cranmore Donkey Sanctuary faded.

The former reptile house was now home to Torsten's scale model of Bavaria, which he had generously donated. All day he patiently let kids start and stop the trains. He periodically gave live demonstrations of how he built new features of the landscape, and even the model animals for the park.

Nan baked cakes two at a time and had recruited her husband – who the staff affectionately knew as Gramps – to sell them. He had a mobile refreshment stand that he could pedal around the park. Mariella had welded it together from the tandem, adding an electric motor from a washing machine so it zoomed around effortlessly.

Gorilla Kingdom had a huge hole in the fence and a warning sign above it saying:

Enter at your own risk.

Wooden ladders and rope bridges were suspended between trees, with dozens of little tree houses and platforms to play on. There was even a large bulldozer to climb in and beep the horn. Kids spent hours there swinging on ropes and racing around the enclosure. Every now and then, Gorilla Man would emerge from his cabin and chase them around the treetops, hurling bananas and thumping his chest.

Tortoise Town was popular with younger kids, who clambered into giant fibreglass shells with their limbs and heads protruding from holes. The human-tortoises crawled in and around little caves and giant lettuce leaves. Every so often, a parent would have to climb over the wall to rescue their child who had flipped onto their back and got stuck, or simply curled up inside their shell for a nap.

Another field housed Daft Giraffes, where six people at a time would balance on stilts whilst wearing an enormous giraffe head. Inside the costumes, the person could see out of the animal's eyes far above, using a periscope made of mirrors. Cass had thought of this, inspired by her selfie-stick spy camera. For a moment it would feel to those people as if they were up in the treetops like the tallest animals on earth. Mostly though, they just came tumbling down onto the mattresses below, shrieking with laughter. Seeing a giraffe come crashing down never failed to make Cass laugh.

A zipline linked the yard to the bottom field, and in between gorilla chases, John tirelessly helped kids and grownups to don a pair of wings and a mask that enabled binocular hawk vision. They squealed with delight as he sent them hurtling across the park.

The sloth was now hidden somewhere different every day, and visitors spent hours searching trees and buildings for it. In time, Torsten had plans to create ten different camouflaged animals to find in the park, like an ever-evolving treasure hunt. He couldn't sleep at night thinking about how to make a chameleon that could actually change colour.

On the opening day, Rosie came running up to Mariella. "Mum, look over there. It's Cobra Lady! It's definitely her. I recognise those white jeans!"

The family of three who a month ago had been ushered out of the park with the threat of a wild cobra noticed Rosie and Mariella looking at them and came striding over.

"I came for a selfie," said their daughter, Ashleigh.

"Oh yes, sure. Lily is over there and there's a little queue, but it won't take long," said Mariella.

The girl looked a bit confused, so her mum interjected. "No, she means with you! You're her hero, Mariella. We saw you on live TV on that zebra, telling those men what for. Ash has got a picture of you on her wall. She made us print out the bit where Lily smashed the sign!"

"Oh, right! Wow. Come on then." Mariella blushed as she posed for what would become the first of many selfies that day, and then the young family headed off towards Bavaria.

Mariella looked at Rosie and said, "Go on! We have to do it now! It'll be too funny!" Rosie smiled and ran towards the office. A few minutes later, an announcement came over the loudspeakers in the yard with a familiar nasal voice.

"This is a customer announcement. There is a COBRA loose in the park. Run for your lives!"

A stable door swung open and out shot a snake. It was L-shaped, with a body trailed across the ground the length of a bicycle, and a tall neck that stood the height of a five-year-old child. The modified boa constrictor still had its tongue poking in and out, but now it was painted black and had a large cobra hood. On wheels hidden on the underside of its belly it raced forwards, controlled remotely by Torsten from his workshop. Kids and adults screamed and laughed as the enormous snake blasted around the yard, periodically squirting out water from its fangs.

"Your zoo rocks!" Ashleigh shouted as she ran past Mariella.

Chapter 36

Final Payment

The last two weeks of the summer holidays flew by in a blur of newspaper interviews, selfies and general chaos. The money rolled in, and four days before the deadline, Mariella saw that the total had already soared past the £40,000 she owed to the bank.

BBC Hampshire continued dropping in to keep up with the story and asked to be there when Mariella made the final payment to the bank.

Knightwood Bank had received a lot of flak on social media for its awful treatment of Mariella. They were keen to introduce to the world their new branch manager, Priyanka, and make it clear that Peter was no longer with the company.

Mariella and John proudly handed over the cheque and signed papers to Priyanka on live television. The park was officially theirs. Priyanka humbly apologised for all their previous troubles and assured them that Knightwood Bank would be more than happy to support them in future if they needed it.

Occasionally Mariella would hear Leo roar next door, but she had not heard from his owner Elvin since the golf course incident. Former employees had come out of the woodwork to say how awful McEadly had been as a boss, and how badly he treated the animals. McZoo currently stood at a one-star rating on Tripadvisor, ranking it the very worst of "Things to do with kids in Westingbury".

Knockoff Zoo was a major hit, and Mariella was inundated with offers from entertainment companies to create more Knockoff Zoos around the UK and beyond. She was even nominated for Businessperson of the Year, but lost to a person who had invented a left-handed potato peeler.

Right now, she just wanted to kick off her red wellies and be with Rosie, who had just a few more days before school restarted for the autumn term.

"You did this, Rosie," she said as she gazed out of the window one evening. "There were so many points this summer that I really thought it was impossible, and it was always you who gave me the power to keep going."

Rosie hugged her mum as they watched the park close up and its staff make their way to their cars to leave for the end of the day. John was last to go, checking the sheds were padlocked and finally walking across the yard away from the bungalow. Rosie went to say goodbye to her dad, but Mariella stopped her and went to the front door herself, opening it wide.

"Where do you think you're going?" she shouted.

"Home!" he called back.

"Well, come on then," Mariella said.

John froze for a minute and looked confused, before walking towards the bungalow with a huge grin.

"Are you sure?" he asked as he got to the door.

"Get in." She smiled affectionately. "Dinner isn't gonna cook itself."

Rosie jumped off the sofa and ran towards her parents, and the family hugged each other like three fish fingers in a sandwich.

Also by James DuBern

Six Canadian teens visit the sub-Arctic wilderness to view polar bears. They become snowbound in a fort with its terrifying owner, Mr Lagrave. With escape attempts thwarted, Lance and his schoolmates must find the courage to face him and the massive polar bear which terrorises the estate.

Author's note

Thanks so much for finishing *Wild Summer*. I hope you enjoyed reading it as much as I enjoyed writing it. If you have time, it would mean the world to me if you could rate or review this book on Amazon.

I live in Hampshire (like Mariella!) and this was my first book. I've subsequently written a series called *World's Deadliest School Trips*, which you can also find on Amazon.

Thanks to my wonderful family for helping me with this book. I couldn't have written it without you.

Made in the USA
Middletown, DE
31 August 2023